"Jake, what would you say about having a baby?" Maggie blurted.

"A baby?" Jake blinked, obviously startled by the abrupt question.

"Your baby," she prompted expectantly—knowing she was doing this all wrong—but she couldn't hold back now.

"My baby?" he echoed softly, and his eyes darkened a fraction of a second before he brought the shutters down. "Look, Maggie, I know you were badly let down, and that the two of us…went a bit further than we should have that night. But I told you up-front that I won't be getting married."

"But I wasn't asking you to marry me," she retorted, completely sidetracked. She suddenly realized that he still hadn't commented on her announcement, and wondered if she hadn't made herself clear. "Jake, I just wanted to tell you that we—"

"I'm sorry, but I'm just not cut out to be a family man."

Dear Reader,

As a member of a large family, I have always been fascinated by the differences between brothers and sisters, even though they share the same basic genetic makeup. Even their relationships with their parents can be very different.

In Maggie ffrench's case, the feeling of always being second-best to her parents didn't affect the love she had for her brother, David. She even followed him into medicine in a subconscious attempt to get her parents' appreciation, but discovered that she actually loved it! Her career became important to how she felt about herself. Yet, despite working long hours in a busy E.R. department, she still longed to have a loving family of her own.

As soon as Maggie met E.R. consultant Jake Lascelles, she knew he was the perfect candidate with whom to start that family. Jake was the man of her dreams—except he made it clear that he would never be a "happy families" man. So she had to settle for friendship.

And now, with her brother having troubles of his own on the other side of the world, when her latest attempt at *forever* collapses, it's Jake's shoulder Maggie finds herself crying on, knowing she'll never stop loving him.

Look out for David's story later in the year.

I hope you enjoy getting to know the ffrench doctors as much as I enjoyed writing about them.

Happy reading!

Josie

His
Longed-For
Baby

Josie Metcalfe

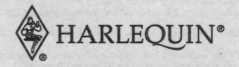

TORONTO • NEW YORK • LONDON
AMSTERDAM • PARIS • SYDNEY • HAMBURG
STOCKHOLM • ATHENS • TOKYO • MILAN • MADRID
PRAGUE • WARSAW • BUDAPEST • AUCKLAND

ISBN 0-373-06503-5

HIS LONGED-FOR BABY

First North American Publication 2005

CHAPTER ONE

'YOU'LL just have to find yourself another wife, Liam...' Maggie said in a voice that shook with something more than mere anger.

Ordinarily, she hated drawing attention to herself, but she was so incensed that she barely noticed the increasingly fascinated stares of the party-goers surrounding them.

'If you'd told me you just wanted someone to take care of your children, I could have helped you to look for a nanny. As for a wife's other *duties*,' she continued as a scathing finale, 'I'm sure it would be far more economical to pay by the hour—you'd get more variety that way.'

She was vaguely aware that he was purple with embarrassment by the time she turned her back on him and started to make her determined way across the room. By that time, she had begun shaking with reaction and all she wanted to do was disappear into thin air.

What on earth had she done? Had that really been *her* making such a scene? And as for suggesting that he should pay a prosti—

'Hang on, Maggie. I'm coming with you,' Karen muttered in her ear, grabbing her sleeve to halt her progress for a moment. 'I just need to get my coat.'

Maggie didn't even pause. The awful silence was being replaced by whispers and giggles as the colleagues nearest to them reacted to the impromptu entertainment she'd provided for them. It was obvious that almost every eye in the room must have been watching the little drama and she knew she couldn't bear to wait another second to get out.

'Don't bother, Karen,' she said with a brief smile for her friend. 'You might as well enjoy the rest of the evening. I'm just going to go home. I've got some thinking to do.'

And wasn't *that* the understatement of the year? she thought wryly as she hurried back towards the blessed seclusion of her flat, grateful that Karen had finally taken her at her word.

She really didn't think she could take an evening of well-meant sympathy—she was too disgusted with herself.

How could she have been so blind? She'd known Liam for nearly a year now. They'd been engaged for more than three months and she was supposed to have been marrying him tomorrow. How could she *not* have realised that the hospital's up-and-coming cardiothoracic surgeon was nothing more than a liar and a cheat?

An hour later her hands were still trembling with the after-effects of the distasteful scene as she struggled to tie a piece of string around the top of a black plastic rubbish bag.

Someone tapped softly on her door and she froze, hoping that if she stayed still and quiet they would go away. It had to be one of the other people who lived in the house because they were the only ones with a key to get past the main door.

While they didn't all work in the same department, they were all colleagues working at the same hospital and relished the opportunity to let their hair down with a celebration. She'd hoped she'd have the house to herself for a little longer—after all, she knew they'd all accepted her invitation to join her for a drink on the night before her wedding. She'd presumed that the rest would take Karen's lead and stay out enjoying the evening in spite of the fiasco it had turned out to be.

In fact, it was probably Karen out there, she thought with a touch of guilt for ignoring her friend. Hopefully she would go back and join the others because she really didn't want to see anybody until she'd got her thoughts under control.

She gave a silent snort.

'Thoughts? What thoughts?' she muttered under her breath.

She'd been home for an hour and she was still replaying the moment when all her dreams had shattered into dust. For several interminable moments her brain had turned to mush when she'd overheard Liam's gloating conversation with his best man, Jake. Where she'd found the words to throw at her bridegroom-to-be she'd never know, especially when just the thought of them made her hands begin shaking again.

The thing that frightened her most, though, was the thought that she might *not* have overheard Liam— that it might have been years before she'd discovered the full extent of his duplicity.

There was a second tap at the door but she was too wrapped up in the enormity of her lucky escape to pay it much attention.

If Karen hadn't persuaded her that they all ought to go out for a drink this evening...

'Come on, Maggie,' she'd wheedled. 'I know

you're not one to make a big fuss, but at least you can share a drink with the rest of us in the house so we can say our farewells to you. After all, tomorrow you're moving everything to Liam's.' Then, correctly reading Maggie's hesitant agreement before she'd said a word, her friend had quickly added, 'And you *have* to invite our gang from the department, too. We could go to that clubby sort of place that opened up recently on the other side of the high street. It could be an unofficial hen night.'

It had all been so informally arranged that if Maggie hadn't known how much her colleagues relished the chance to escape from the traumas surrounding them in a busy accident and emergency department she'd have been surprised just how the numbers had snowballed.

She supposed she shouldn't have been surprised that Liam and Jake had chosen the same establishment. They'd been friends since they'd met during their medical training, and not only had Liam asked Jake to be his best man but he'd been the person responsible for introducing the two of them in the first place. Anyway, Rendezvous would be the most obvious venue for such a celebration, being in such close proximity to the hospital.

It had been sheer chance that she'd been sitting out of sight on the other side of an over-exuberant arrangement of palm trees and plastic ferns, chatting to Karen while she waited for her specially concocted cocktail—courtesy of the management when they'd discovered that she was getting married in the morning…

If Liam and Jake hadn't stopped to talk on the other side of the same display she wouldn't have been in a position to overhear Jake ask Liam how he'd persuaded his bride-to-be to give up her long-held dream of having a large family.

'It won't be a problem,' she'd heard Liam say, his airy unconcern covering her gasp of disbelief. 'It'll probably take Maggie several years before she twigs that nothing's happening on the pregnancy front, and as I've already had two kids she'll automatically assume that it's her fault. And by the time she's gone through all the tests...'

'You mean you haven't *told* her?' Jake cut in harshly, and the icy anger in his voice raised the hairs on the back of Maggie's neck. She'd rarely heard that edge to his tone and she'd been working with him for nearly two years. Jake Lascelles might be her senior in the accident and emergency department but he couldn't be a more easygoing boss. Right from the first they'd become friends—friendly enough to share middle-of-the-night confidences.

'Have I told Maggie about the vasectomy? No way!' Liam exclaimed jocularly, completely oblivious to Maggie's shocked exclamation. 'She's far too good a prospect to miss out on. The kids love her and she already dotes on them enough for me to know that she'll be happy to keep them out of my hair. Anyway, two rug rats are enough for anyone. With Julia going off like that, I didn't have any choice about getting dumped with custody of them, but I'm not stupid enough to want any more—not with my career taking off the way it is.'

'But you've told her that you're looking forward to having another one as soon as you can—the first of several,' Jake argued.

Maggie could have died on the spot as she heard

her private plans voiced in public. She could remember all too clearly the way she'd happily chattered to Jake during a night-shift lull, confiding that she and Liam were hoping to come back from their honeymoon with their first baby already on the way.

'I bet you'd promise the same thing if you were looking forward to plenty of action on your honeymoon,' Liam joked coarsely. 'Can you imagine it? Because of her scruples about the kids being in the house, the damn woman wouldn't even move in with me until we're married. She's going to be more than willing to share a bed with me if she thinks we're trying to make babies.'

Maggie's ears were filled with the frantic beating of her heart and she wondered whether she was going to be sick. But even though the noise seemed loud enough to fill the room, it didn't drown out Liam's voice as he continued inexorably to demolish all her dreams of happily-ever-after.

'Then, by the time she finds out there's never going to be the patter of tiny feet, the kids will be old enough for me to pack them off to boarding school and I'll be free to play the field again. Not that she'll know what I get up to in the sluices and linen cupboards once she gives up her job to look after the kids, but, then, what the eye doesn't see…'

Maggie felt strangely light-headed as the extent of his duplicity became clear, and she found herself clinging to the edge of the table with white-knuckled fingers, wondering how she'd got herself into such a devastating situation.

Jake had introduced her to his old medical school friend nearly a year ago, and although she'd teased him about trying to be a matchmaker, she'd immediately been impressed by Liam's dedication to his work—the feeling of awe she'd always felt about the complexity of cardiothoracic surgery increasing his stature in her eyes.

He didn't have the charisma or looks that Jake had, neither did he send the same shivers down her spine, but Jake had made it perfectly clear right at the outset that there would only ever be friendship between them, so she'd had to settle for that.

Gradually, over the months of Liam's determined pursuit, respect had grown into something more personal until she'd thought she'd known the man well enough to make the most solemn promises of her life with him.

Obviously she hadn't known him at all, because she'd had no idea that the main reason he'd wanted her was as a nanny for his children, with the added bonus of convenient sex. Of course she knew that few couples these days waited until they were married before sleeping together. In their case, circumstances had played a major part in preventing that happening. Her flat was furnished with an unromantically small bed, and she'd been far too aware of all their colleagues surrounding them to contemplate making love there. And as for any intimacy taking place in Liam's house, she was old-fashioned enough to feel uncomfortable about sleeping with him in his bed before they were married, because his children were in the house.

It was a decidedly chilling thought that if she hadn't had such scruples, he might not even have thought of offering marriage at all.

An hour and a long hot shower later, the sick feeling had abated a little but she still felt strangely hollow inside with a heavy ache around her heart.

One day she'd probably be able to laugh when she remembered the expression on Liam's face when she'd stepped out from behind the plastic flowers. Ellie and Jamie's goldfish—the only pet Liam would let his children have because it required the least effort on his part—had gaped at her just like that last weekend.

The doorbell rang, telling her there was someone calling her from the main door of the house, but she didn't bother buzzing down on the intercom to find out who it was. Her windows weren't visible from the front so no one would know she was there.

Anyway, there wasn't anyone she wanted to see, so there was no point in answering.

At least she could be certain that it wasn't Liam, she thought with a flash of satisfaction as she finally managed to squash her wedding dress tightly enough into the plastic bag to secure some string around the neck of it.

She suffered a momentary pang when she remembered the first time she'd tried the dress on and had turned to look at herself in the panoramic wall of mirrors.

It hadn't been in the least bit what she'd been looking for—the classic winter white suit that Liam had suggested, so that she'd be able to wear it afterwards and get her money's worth out of it.

This dress had been the absolute embodiment of every romantic dream she'd ever had. She hadn't even reached her teens when she'd known that, whatever she achieved in her eventual career, her ultimate goal was to find the man of her dreams and build the close, loving family she'd always wanted.

There were no frills or flounces to detract from the classic simplicity of the fitted bodice or the full-length elegant sleeves and the layer upon layer of sheer silk organza that would caress her body and float behind her in a slow-motion dream as she walked towards her groom.

She straightened up from her self-imposed task and caught sight of herself in the tri-fold mirror on the top of her chest of drawers. She pulled a wry smile at the picture she made, with her face devoid of any trace of make-up and her toffee-coloured hair standing out at odd spiky angles after the rough towelling she'd given it after her shower.

'Not quite the typical picture of the eager bride on the eve of her wedding,' she murmured, and saw her lip quiver as she drew in a shaky breath.

'Don't you dare!' she threatened the figure in the mirror with a glare from eyes that were more green than blue in the lamplight. 'Not one single tear, do you hear me? He's not worth it!'

There was another tap on the door. A different rhythm this time, and she sighed as she wondered who it was. While Liam was unlikely to turn up to apologise, he probably wanted to tell her what he thought of her for making such a scene. He'd certainly been mortified when she'd told him what she thought of him...and in front of so many members of staff, too!

Unfortunately, unless something juicier happened in the meantime, by the time she returned to work the hospital grapevine would probably have blown everything all out of proportion and she would be sharing equally in the notoriety.

Still, that was better than the alternative. It might have been years before she discovered just what sort of man she'd married, by which time she'd probably have been too old to have the baby she'd always wanted.

The knock came again, sharper and more determined, and she had a feeling that, unlike her last visitor, they weren't going to give up. She was going to have to speak to them to make them go away, even if it *was* Liam. She certainly didn't have to let anyone come into the flat, because she just wasn't in the mood for company.

She was already speaking as she released the catch, determined to send her visitor away as she stuck just her head around the edge of the door.

'Look, I'm sorry to be unsociable, but if you don't mind, I'd rather not— *Jake?* What are *you* doing here?'

He was the very last person she'd expected to see standing there and the only one who could actually make the whole situation worse. She'd known from the first day he'd introduced her to Liam that the two men had known each other for years, but she had believed that since she'd come to work in his department at least she and Jake had become friends. It actually hurt that he'd thought so little about her feelings that he hadn't told her about Liam's lies.

'How did you get in?' she snapped. 'I didn't buzz down to release the lock on the front door.'

'I know. That's why I let myself in.' He held up a familiar key. 'I used to live here, remember?'

Yes, she remembered. She'd loved it when he'd

used to live right next door to her…that there had been just a single wall separating her bed from the sexiest man she'd ever met. She'd been devastated when, without a word of warning, he'd suddenly bought a prestigious flat in a recently completed development on the other side of the hospital and moved out. OK, anyone could see that his new place was much nicer than this one, but she'd thought he'd enjoyed the friendly atmosphere here as much as she did.

'What are you doing here?' she demanded bluntly, her feelings less than friendly now.

'You wouldn't answer your door when Karen knocked earlier, and she was worried about you. We both were.'

'*You* were worried about me? I don't think so,' she scoffed, the anger that had accompanied her home from the club re-igniting with a vengeance. 'You certainly weren't worried about me when you hatched your little scheme with Liam. How could you be part of such a shabby trick, Jake? I know you trained together, and you were going to be Liam's best man, but I thought at least you were my *friend*.'

'I *am* your friend,' he insisted heatedly, and for just a moment she was almost convinced by the expression of hurt she glimpsed in his eyes. Then he glanced over his shoulder towards the sudden sound of voices down by the front door and the illusion was gone. 'Please, Maggie, could I come in? Some of the gang has obviously come back from the club and… Look, I need to explain and I can't do it out here.'

'There isn't anything to explain,' she said firmly, and began to swing the door shut. If he didn't leave soon she was going to embarrass herself by bursting into tears, no matter how determined she was not to give in. Her only hope was to hold onto the anger until he went. 'Are you forgetting that I overheard your conversation with Liam? It was perfectly obvious that you knew all about his grubby little plan—'

'Maggie, please...don't!' he interrupted, quickly bracing one hand on the door to prevent her closing it in his face. 'Please! You've got to believe me. I honestly didn't know that Liam hadn't—' He broke off as the chattering voices came closer; clearly people were on their way up the stairs.

He took a step closer, his hazel eyes darkening with entreaty under the rakish length of the dark hair that always seemed to be just a few days beyond the haircut he never remembered to write in his diary.

'Please, Maggie? Just two minutes?'

There was something in his eyes, a quiet plea that she didn't think she would ever be able to resist. How could she when she'd lost her heart to him the first time they'd met? Unfortunately, that had been before she'd learned that he was the one man she could never have.

Silently, she stepped back and pulled the door wider, her turbulent emotions making her undecided whether she was making another stupid mistake.

Almost as if he was afraid she would change her mind, he swung the door swiftly closed behind him and leant back against it.

It wasn't until she saw his gaze slide over her that she remembered that she was wearing nothing more than her ratty old towelling robe—the one she'd been going to throw away in the morning at the start of her new life.

He, on the other hand, still looked as though he

could model for the next issue of *GQ* in his neatly pressed black chinos, black leather jacket and a deep blue shirt that almost matched his eyes. At least his dark hair was as unruly as ever, but whether that was just from the chilly breeze that had sprung up earlier in the evening or from his perennial habit of running his fingers through it, she didn't know.

For a moment there was silence between them, the only sound the chatter of the other residents passing on their way along the corridor.

Maggie wasn't sure if it was a sign of paranoia but she was almost certain she heard their tone change as they went past her door. Were they talking about her…about the scene she'd made? The whole hospital was probably going to be talking about it by tomorrow, the tale growing with every telling.

Well, there was nothing she could do about it now.

'So,' she said briskly. 'The clock's ticking on your two minutes. What did you want to tell me?'

Unable to stand still while she waited for a reply, she threaded her way between the neat stacks of cardboard boxes containing all her worldly goods across to the mini-kitchen in the corner of the room to fill the kettle.

Behind her there was a sharp rustling, tearing sound and a muttered curse.

'Damn. I'm sorry, Maggie. I tripped over this bag and— Oh, damn!' he ended on a stricken note.

She turned to find him holding the plastic bag into which she'd just struggled to stuff her once-in-a-lifetime wedding dress—the wedding dress that was now spilling out of a gaping hole in the side like the silky entrails of some alien life form.

She closed her eyes against the sight and turned

back to her task, trying for a note of unconcern as she spoke over her shoulder. 'Throw it in the corner by the door, will you? There are several other bags of rubbish to go out to the bins before I leave in the morning.'

'Oh, Maggie, you shouldn't have done this to your wedding dress...' Jake began, but she barely registered more than the dismay in his voice as a sudden thought struck her.

'My God, Jake, I'm supposed to be moving out tomorrow!' she exclaimed in horror as she whirled to face him. 'I'm going to have nowhere to live!'

'If you phone the letting agents first thing in the morning, would they let you stay on? Could you renew your contract?'

'Impossible,' she said glumly. 'You know one-bedroom flats are at a premium this close to the hospital, especially affordable ones. They had a list as long as your arm of people waiting to snap it up and the contracts have all been signed.'

'Too true. You'd probably be murdered by the next tenant if you refused to move out.'

'Oh, thanks! That really makes me feel better,' she grumbled as she finished dumping half a spoonful of sugar in his black coffee and a splash of milk in her own.

She turned to find that, in the absence of anywhere else to sit, he'd perched on the arm of her only comfortable chair.

She groaned and handed him the steaming mug before sinking to the floor to lean back against a pile of cartons. 'Everything's such a mess, Jake. Not just about the flat but my whole life.'

She heard him sigh heavily but didn't dare look up

at him, It was taking all her concentration to control the urge to weep all over his shoulder, something she'd never done in all the time she'd known him—even after a particularly traumatic day.

Unfortunately, even that possibility was gone now. She'd lost her heart to him so quickly, so deeply, that it had taken her a long time to force herself to think of him as nothing more than her department head who also happened to be her friend. After today's revelations, she wasn't sure whether he was friend or foe, but his was still the only ear she wanted when she needed to offload her troubles.

But first he had some questions to answer.

'So, Jake, tell me…did you have any intention of warning me that Liam was lying and cheating his way into marriage?' she demanded. 'I bet the two of you were having a good laugh at the stupid, gullible twit who actually believed someone would want to marry her and have a family with her.'

'No, Maggie!' he exclaimed sharply, clearly startled by the idea. 'God, no! It wasn't like that.'

'So what *was* it like?' She knew her chin was tilted up at what he'd christened her don't-mess-with-me angle, but that was what she felt like at this moment. Well, it was either that or sob her heart out, and she did still have *some* pride. 'Don't forget, Jake, I was privy to a very revealing conversation behind that scaled-down version of Kew Gardens. I *know* that he'd told you about his vasectomy and that you chose not to tell me. Why? Is it all part of the male solidarity thing?'

'Well, yes, I knew about the vasectomy,' he admitted roughly. The way he was staring at his white-knuckled grip on the handle of the mug showed that he was clearly uncomfortable with the direction of the conversation, but she hardened her heart.

Then his eyes swung up to meet hers and the searing honesty in his hazel gaze was unmistakable. 'But, Maggie, I promise that I only found out about it a few days ago, totally by accident. Tonight, when I realised that he hadn't told you... You *did* hear that part, didn't you?' he demanded, only continuing when she nodded, relieved to find that he was still the forthright man she knew.

'I was so angry with him,' he growled fiercely. 'I've known right from when you first came to work in A and E that your dream was to have a big family, and I was asking Liam how he'd persuaded you to give up all your plans. I was so surprised that you'd changed your mind—that you'd decided you would be happy to look after just his two.'

Now that she thought about it, the conversation she'd overheard had sounded something like that.

Maggie sighed as some of the knots inside her loosened a fraction. It was bad enough to find out that the man she was going to marry had deceived her from the beginning. The thought that someone she'd counted as a friend had been part of the deception had been too much heartbreak for one day.

'And anyway,' he continued gruffly, 'the last thing I'd call you was stupid and gullible. You're the most warm-hearted, generous person I know.'

'With the most abysmal instincts about men,' she added wryly, even as she basked in the unexpected testimonial. 'How could I have been so wrong about Liam?'

'Perhaps because he was careful to tell you only what you wanted to hear?' Jake suggested quietly.

'Hey, don't beat yourself up about it or you'll make me feel even more guilty—after all, I knew how much you were looking forward to starting a family and I was the one who introduced you. You *must* know I'd never have done it if I'd known he'd had the op.'

It didn't take more than a glance at him to know that he meant that. And she *did* know that he wouldn't have done such a thing. He was far too honest to play stupid games like that.

'I suppose that next you'll be telling me that I should be grateful to you for showing me his true colours *before* we tied the knot,' she retorted, more relieved than she could say that she hadn't lost her friend after all.

She allowed herself to relax a little, unaccountably pleased that the two of them hadn't lost the rapport they'd developed over the last two years. She had several female friends with whom she enjoyed sharing girl talk, but Jake was different. With him she felt so at ease that she didn't have to think twice before she spoke her mind, knowing he would understand what she meant. Some of their colleagues in the department were all too ready to take offence at the slightest thing or, worse, to spread gossip…

'Oh, Lord!' she groaned, dropping her head down to her knees as a less than happy thought crossed her mind. 'I'm going to have to get another job.'

'What? Why on earth would you want to do that?' he demanded. 'You and Liam don't even work in the same department. He only comes down if we need him to consult over a patient.'

'That may be so, but you know as well as I do that A and E is staffed by some of the biggest gossips in the hospital, and most of the ones off duty were invited to the club for a drink tonight. You wait. By the morning, the hospital will be absolutely buzzing with the most amazing rumours about why the wedding's been called off.'

It was Jake's turn to groan. 'There'll be everything from abduction by aliens to…God knows what! Hey, perhaps I could get people to bet on it. Perhaps we could make a bit of money out of this!'

He let out a startled 'Ouch!' when she aimed a blow at his patella with the side of her hand and nearly toppled him from his precarious perch on the arm of the chair.

'Don't you dare stir everything up!' she warned. 'The less anyone says, the sooner it'll all be forgotten.'

Forgotten by everyone but her, she added silently, then remembered the two innocent little faces who were the other victims in this fiasco.

'Oh, Jake!' she exclaimed. 'What about Ellie and Jamie? They were so excited about being my attendants—having their day in the limelight all dressed up to the nines. They're going to be heartbroken when they wake up in the morning and Liam tells them it's all off.'

'It can't be helped…unless you're willing to go through with the wedding just to stop them being disappointed?'

'Of course not, you idiot,' she retorted instantly. When he put it like that, it was obvious. 'I wouldn't marry Liam if he was the last man on earth.'

Jake didn't comment, and the longer he was quiet the heavier the silence seemed to grow.

'What?' she demanded with a frown, needing to

know what had put that disapproving expression on his face.

'Well, I'm just a bit…surprised how quickly you can change your mind about someone,' he said seriously. 'Just a few hours ago he was the love of your life and your husband-to-be, and now he's the last man on earth you'd marry.'

His delivery was quiet-voiced enough to sound off-hand but landed with the weight of condemnation. Not that she needed him to pile on the guilt. Perhaps this was the time for her to purge her conscience.

'He was never the love of my life,' she admitted uncomfortably, deliberately avoiding looking at him in case he was as good at reading her mind as he seemed to be with his patients.

'What?' Now he sounded genuinely shocked. 'Then why the blazes were you going to marry him?'

'Because he asked me!' she retorted flippantly, anxious to avoid delving into deeper waters. Jake's friendship was all she could ever have of him and she wasn't going to risk losing that by admitting that *he* was the man she loved. It was far safer to steer the conversation to other waters. 'And also because I'll be thirty on my next birthday and I didn't want to wait too much longer before I had the first of those babies I've been wanting all my life.'

'So your biological clock's ticking, and you won't be content just to bring up someone else's babies,' he charged grimly. 'What would you have done if you'd married someone without children and then found out that he couldn't father any of his own? I suppose you'd have divorced him and gone looking for someone else.'

A tiny alarm sounded in her head at the unexpected

vehemence in his tone but, as Liam's long-time friend, she supposed he was bound to see things from the man's point of view.

'Not at all!' she exclaimed, stung by the implications that she would be so fickle. 'I'm *not* just looking for a sperm donor. I want a real marriage to a man I can respect and trust. I thought I'd found that, but even as his friend you have to admit that underneath that charming exterior Liam falls a long way short on every count.'

Unable to sit still any longer, she scrambled to her feet, but there was no room to pace off her returning anger.

'I'm making another cup of coffee. This one's gone cold,' she muttered, needing to do something to ward off the heated prickle of tears that had suddenly tried to overwhelm her.

Was that really what Jake thought of her? Did he honestly see her as someone willing to marry just for what she wanted to get out of the relationship? Didn't he know that she'd already cared deeply for little Ellie and Jamie and would have loved them just as much as any babies she carried?

She blinked furiously, forbidding a single tear to fall, while she switched the kettle on. She had far too much to think about to waste time on crying.

For example, there was the matter of cancelling the fortnight's honeymoon she'd paid for—Liam still hadn't paid her for his share and she had no idea whether she would be able to make a claim on her holiday insurance to recover the money. Then there was the problem of finding herself somewhere to live now that she wouldn't be moving in with Liam. What were the chances that she'd have somewhere by this time tomorrow? With all the money she'd spent on her dress and the honeymoon she couldn't afford to splash out on a hotel, so she could very well end up out on the street...

She'd been so involved with her thoughts that she hadn't heard Jake moving around. The first time she realised that he was standing right behind her was when she swung round with two steaming mugs in her hand and splattered the scalding liquid over both of them.

Jake swore rawly even as he reached out to pull the sodden towelling robe away from her skin. 'Dammit, Maggie, I'm sorry. I thought you knew I was there.'

'It's all over your shirt!' she exclaimed, ignoring the searing heat against her own flesh in her efforts to undo his shirt buttons with shaking fingers. 'You need to get cold water on it to take the heat out.'

Suddenly, without any warning, he scooped her up in his arms to hurry towards her tiny bathroom.

'Forget about me,' he growled as he dumped her unceremoniously in the shower cubicle and reached for the taps. 'My skin's far tougher than yours.'

She gasped as the water hit her like an icy wall, then gasped again when he finally managed to wrench the heavily sodden fabric off her shoulders.

Distracted by her efforts to try to wrest the first of his shirt buttons through their holes, she shrugged the restricting dressing-gown off her shoulders and it fell to the floor of the cubicle with a resounding slap.

With the impact of the icy water on her totally naked body Maggie froze, her eyes wide with the shocked realisation that she was standing in front of Jake without a stitch to cover her blushes.

'Oh, Maggie,' she heard him whisper, and when she saw the heat of desire turn his hazel eyes to molten gold as they roamed her naked body from head to toe, suddenly she wasn't cold any more.

She reached out trembling hands towards his shirt again, half expecting him to stop her, then whimpered in frustration when she found she couldn't force the little discs through their respective holes anyway.

'I can't do this!' she complained. 'And I want to see you, too.'

His eyes met hers, the heat in them fierce enough to turn cold water into steam, and her arousal was so intense it was almost pain.

It had never felt like this before, even though she'd desired Jake from the first moment she'd met him.

'Maggie, you don't want to do this,' he was warning her, even as he was stripping his shirt over his head. 'It's just the result of the shock of being scalded coming on top of the scene in the club.'

Her only response was to reach for his head with both hands, sliding her fingers through his hair to pull him closer.

'If you don't want to make love with me, then say so,' she said, her steady words totally at odds with her trembling body. She was very afraid that he would be able to see her vulnerability in her eyes but she couldn't look away.

'It's not that I don't want to…' he denied quickly, but she wasn't reassured—not when he wouldn't meet her eyes properly. Had she read him so wrong? Was it just because she'd never wanted anything as much as she wanted this, that she was presuming that he felt the same way?

'Jake!' She heard the pleading in her voice but after

two long years of wanting him it didn't really matter. 'I need you,' she whispered, the words almost lost in the sound of the freezing torrent as her teeth started to chatter and she reached for the fastening of his waistband.

Whatever reservations he may have had disappeared completely then. In moments, he was stepping back into the cubicle and her heart soared as he reached for her.

'Kiss me!' he growled as he wrapped his arms around her in the confined space, but she was already tilting her face up towards him.

It was everything she'd dreamed of and more—hot, sweet, fierce and every bit as ravenous as she could have wished.

'Please!' she whimpered, tightening her grasp so that her slick flesh slid against his in a graphic illustration of her need for more.

'Hold tight,' he ordered, and he bent to lift her, his hands cupping her bottom.

Without any prompting she wrapped her legs around his waist and when she felt him press against her intimate heat she trembled in anticipation of what was to come.

'Oh, Maggie!' he groaned, and she was certain that she felt him quivering with the same onslaught of pleasure. Then he turned to brace her against the tiled wall of the cubicle, leaning back just far enough to gaze his fill at the way they fitted in each other's arms.

He was so broad and strong against her slighter frame, his muscles and sinews standing out in stark relief as he supported her, every swell and hollow slick with rivulets of water that eventually disappeared between their bodies.

'Give me your breast,' he demanded hoarsely.

She hesitated momentarily, stunned to feel everything inside her clenching in response to his raw command. Lack of experience made her waver, but a glimpse of uncertainty in his gaze was enough to restore her courage and she cupped one hand around herself and offered her breast up to him.

He nuzzled his face against her and the smoothness of his jaw told her that he must have shaved recently. He was so warm against the chill of her skin that she was briefly reminded about the necessity of taking the heat out of their recent scalds, then he opened his mouth to take her inside and nothing else mattered.

She'd never dreamed that she would be so in tune with him, every move so well choreographed as if they'd already been lovers in fact rather than in her imagination. Finally, when she could bear his teasing torment no longer, she took control, tightening her legs around him as she impaled herself to the hilt and shattered around him with a high keening cry.

Even as her body clenched rhythmically around him she felt him follow her into the maelstrom, and he gave a wordless shout of ecstasy as his release exploded into her secret depths.

For several moments it seemed as if neither of them could have moved if they'd wanted to, their arms wrapped tightly around each other as they panted for breath. Maggie was absolutely certain that if Jake hadn't been pressing her against the tiled wall she would have slid bonelessly down its slick surface into the puddle in the bottom of the bath.

She was totally stunned. Was this what she'd been

missing all these years? Or was it something special, just between the two of them? She chuckled when she realised that there was only one way to find out.

'Wow! What do you do for an encore?'

'Encore?' Was that disbelief in his voice? It was hard to tell when his face was buried in the curve between her neck and shoulder. 'I'm still waiting to find out if I've survived the overture.'

She gripped her legs around his waist then squeezed the muscles that surrounded him where he was still buried deep inside her. She laughed again, a throaty, husky sound that she'd never heard herself make before, when she felt the burgeoning proof of his returning arousal.

'Take it from me,' she whispered, 'you've definitely survived. I've got the evidence to prove it.' And she deliberately tightened her internal muscles around him again.

He groaned, apparently helpless to stop himself thrusting in response, and she felt a surge of feminine power.

'You say you've got evidence?' he demanded hoarsely, finally straightening up enough to meet her eyes. 'Well, how about taking this somewhere warmer and drier to explore that evidence?'

CHAPTER TWO

WHAT had he done? What on earth had he been thinking about? his brain screamed at him the next morning when Jake woke up to find Maggie still spread-eagled limply across his body.

'Down, boy!' he muttered when his body reacted all too eagerly to her soft curves. *It* knew exactly what had happened during the night and was only too willing for it to happen again. The fact that it was something he'd wanted for the last two years had nothing to do with it. He'd known right from the first that he and Maggie could never be more than friends.

It was precisely because she was a friend that he'd come to try to talk to her. He'd been worried about her. Worried about the fact that, at a time he would expect a woman to need the support of a female friend, she was refusing to answer her door to Karen. Worried about her state of mind, knowing how much she'd been looking forward to being a mother to Liam's two children and concerned about her reaction to the destruction of her dream of having a houseful of her own.

Not that he'd thought for a moment that she would do anything stupid or life-threatening—she had her feet far too firmly on the ground for that. And besides, he knew from working with her in the A and E department that she valued human life too highly to contemplate taking her own.

Still, he'd been concerned enough to make the trek

to her door, utilising the spare key he'd forgotten to hand over to his successor when he'd moved out...

He gave a silent snort of derision when he realised that he wasn't fooling himself with *that* tale. He hadn't forgotten to hand over the key at all. Something inside him had wanted to hang onto it as the last tangible evidence that he'd once lived next to Maggie ffrench, had slept just inches away from her on the other side of a wall that was so poorly sound-proofed that he'd been convinced he could hear her every time she turned over in her sleep. And if that wasn't a pathetic admission for a rational adult man, then nothing was.

If he hadn't been so concerned about her, then the way she'd greeted him at the door last night—spitting like an angry cat—would have made him laugh.

She wasn't a big woman by any means—at least a head shorter than he was in her stockinged feet—and she was slender and willowy, too, but she obviously didn't see that as a reason to back down in an argument. There had been more than one obstreperous patient who had discovered that about the petite A and E doctor to his cost, drunkard or bully or both.

The fact that she'd stood her ground last night had relieved him on one score—she wasn't going to allow her aborted marriage to defeat her spirit, even though it seemed to have dented her belief in their friendship.

But when he'd stripped her coffee-soaked dressing-gown off her last night and seen her standing in the shower, every slender inch of her naked, every curve gleaming with rivulets of water while she'd struggled with his shirt buttons...

It had been every erotic dream he'd had over the last two years come to life in front of him...everything he'd ever wanted since the day he'd first met her...everything he knew he couldn't have...

It would have been all right if she hadn't still been trembling so much, her eyes wide with shock. A scalding cup of coffee tipped over her had obviously been one trauma too many after the evening's revelations.

He'd recognised the combination of hurt and vulnerability in those fascinating blue-green eyes, but it had been the unexpected desire he'd seen blossoming in their widely dilated pupils that had sent his common sense scattering to the winds.

He knew there could never be a permanent relationship between the two of them, had known ever since the first time he'd seen the eagerness in her face when she'd spoken about the family she wanted to have one day. The trouble was, in spite of the attraction between them, he knew he could never be what she wanted...what she needed.

The fact that she was everything that *he'd* ever wanted and needed just didn't come into it. He'd known for years that his career was going to be the most important part of his life and there was nothing he could do to change that. It was far too late.

When she woke up he was going to have to find the words to tell her that this was all there could be between them.

Find the words? Ha! As if there *were* words to put a pretty face on the fact that this was going to have to be a one-night stand. A totally out-of-this-world, mind-blowing, one-of-a-kind one-night stand that, no matter how utterly perfect it had been, was going to leave him laden with guilt for the rest of his life.

What sort of man was he? How could he have

given in to temptation when he'd known how vulnerable she was? It didn't matter that he'd desired her for two long years—*she* didn't know that. He'd made very certain that she understood that he could only offer friendship.

Oh, but it was so tempting to pretend for just a little bit longer that there could be a more intimate relationship between them. It was just too easy to lift his head a little bit to look all the way down Maggie's slender back to the perfect twin curves of her bottom.

He knew, now, how well those curves fitted his hands, and would remember for ever the husky purring sound she made in her throat when he tightened his grip on them to brace her for his possession.

He stifled a groan of his own when he felt his body responding anew to the graphic thought. She was still asleep, for heaven's sake! She was going to think he was a sex maniac on some sort of hormonal overload if he carried on like this, certainly not a mature thirty-three-year-old who should know better. And the fact that this was the first time he'd been to bed with a woman since he'd met Maggie was no excuse either.

As if she was picking up the intensity of his thoughts, Maggie began to stir, her silky flesh sliding over his rougher planes with a thoroughly arousing friction as she woke.

'Mmm, nice,' she murmured huskily against his throat as she angled her hips against him, clearly only too willing to continue where they'd left off when she'd finally fallen asleep.

His soul-searching ground to an instant halt. Gone were all thoughts of telling her that this couldn't happen again when it obviously was.

Without him even having to think about it, his

hands were already cupping her, stroking her, positioning her for his—

'Jake?' Suddenly, she was stiffening against him. 'Is that your pager?'

He'd been totally deaf to anything but her soft murmurs and the blood pounding through his veins, but now he could hear the wretched thing, too.

'I don't believe it!' he groaned as he dropped his head back on the pillow, squeezing his eyes tight shut against the enticing view.

'It can't be mine,' she reasoned. 'I didn't bring one home with me because I'm not on duty for two weeks.'

'Well, I'm not due on for hours yet,' he growled in frustration. If this was all he was ever going to have of Maggie, he really didn't want anyone or anything interrupting...

The ringing of Maggie's phone halted his unhappy thoughts.

'We'll just have to remember where we were, so we can take up where we left off,' she suggested with a fascinating blush—a blush that amazed him when he remembered all the things the two of them had done since he'd joined her in the shower last night. He'd never had such a generous lover before, or such an eager one, and if he allowed himself to think about all he would be missing for the rest of his life without Maggie in it, he would probably want to slit his throat.

He would just have to settle for slitting the throat of whoever had misread the on-duty roster and dialled *his* number instead.

He padded across the room to retrieve the insistent thing from his trouser pocket.

'Whoever this is, I'll get them off the line as soon as possible so you can make your call,' Maggie said, modestly tugging the duvet over herself with one hand as she reached for the phone with the other.

When he saw her disappear behind thoroughly rumpled cotton Jake stifled another groan. The mood had been well and truly broken now, and that dreaded 'this shouldn't have happened' conversation was suddenly imminent.

'Hi, Karen!' Maggie said, and he grimaced at the thought that he was probably going to have to work out what to say to Maggie's friend, too. After all, Karen knew that he'd intended speaking to Maggie last night, and if she found out that he'd spent the night...

'No, you didn't wake me. What can I do for—? Oh, no!' she exclaimed suddenly, dragging him out of his tangled thoughts. 'Of course I'll come in—I'm not doing anything important today after all. I should be there in twenty minutes. Thirty at the most.'

'What's going on?' Jake demanded as she cut the call and handed the phone to him, apparently unaware that she'd let the bedclothes fall to her lap during her phone call. He was so busy admiring her sweet curves that he almost missed what she was saying.

'Major incident—traffic pile-up on the motorway. Multiple traumas on their way in so they're rounding up all the staff they can reach,' she added with a nod towards his pager.

It didn't take long for Jake to confirm that he too would get to the hospital as soon as he could. If the estimates for the number of casualties were right, this was going to be a day in hell.

He reached for his clothes, sparing a longing

thought for the luxury of a long hot shower. Unfortunately, there was going to be no time for that, and certainly no time for that serious discussion he'd been going to have with Maggie.

'Did you walk or drive last night?' she asked suddenly.

'Walked,' he called back as he scrabbled around in the bathroom, trying to find his other shoe. Thank goodness he would be able to change out of his wrinkled clothes as soon as he reached the hospital. A night on a damp bathroom floor hadn't done them any favours. 'Liam insisted he was going to buy me a drink.'

'And you never drive after you've had alcohol,' she finished for him, something they'd long ago discovered they both believed in. 'Drat! I forgot that. I was hoping you could give me a lift, for speed.'

'We'll just have to run to save time,' he said distractedly, wondering how his second shoe had ended up by the fridge. He was certain he'd been wearing both of them when he'd walked into the bathroom last night, and he definitely hadn't bothered walking around her flat with a shoe in his hand since then. He'd had far more interesting things to—

That was enough!

The night was well and truly over now, all bar the post-mortem. There was no point in tormenting himself with full-colour replays when he was going to need every scrap of concentration to help his patients.

'Ready to go?' he called, checking that he'd put his pager back in his pocket just as Maggie emerged from the bathroom fully clothed and obviously set for action.

*   *   *

At the last moment Maggie suddenly worried that it might not be a good idea for people to see her arriving for work with Jake. The last thing she needed was to give the hospital grapevine something else to get their teeth into. At least Jake could blame the state of his clothes on the downpour outside.

In the event, the whole department was already working to such a pitch that the only notice anyone took of the two of them was to set them to work the moment they arrived.

'Thank God you're both here!' Senior Sister Lina Mackey said when she caught sight of them. 'Can you go to Resus Two? We've already got three beds going in One and another ambulance due any second with a tension pneumothorax on board.'

'Can you give us thirty seconds to change into scrubs?' Jake asked, his long legs already taking him towards the locker room at a rapid clip.

If she'd had her way, Maggie thought as she pulled the faded green cotton top over her head and tight-ened the baggy drawstring waist on the matching trousers, she wouldn't have been working in the same room as Jake. She'd barely had time to draw breath since she'd woken up this morning and it didn't look as if it was going to get any better. Even so, working in the close proximity that such a multiple trauma scenario demanded wouldn't give her the space to put her thoughts and feelings into order.

What on earth had possessed her last night? She'd never been so brazen in her life. Even now, remem-bering the way she'd given up on taking his coffee-soaked clothes off his body and had dragged him fully clothed to join her in the shower cubicle made her whole body grow hot.

And this definitely wasn't the time or the place for such thoughts, not when their patients were going to be fighting for their very lives.

The fact that she and Jake had spent the night together mustn't be allowed to interfere with the way the two of them worked together.

Both of them reached Resus Two before their first patient, but only just.

Swiftly, she grabbed two disposable plastic aprons and thrust one in his direction before pulling hers over her head and wrapping the ties around her waist. She reached for the box of small disposable gloves, her hand colliding with Jake's as he reached across her for the larger size.

'Sorry,' she muttered, horrified to feel a sudden wash of heat surge into her cheeks. For heaven's sake! What was the matter with her? They'd been brushing against each other over and over again for the last two years without a problem. Was she going to blush every time now?

Concentrate! she reminded herself, grateful to find the paramedic's report far more urgent than her own petty worries.

'ABCs were relatively normal when we reached him,' the young woman reported briskly, referring to the notes on her clipboard. 'But he'd been trapped in his seat by the steering-wheel when the whole front of his vehicle collapsed towards him. While he was being cut out of the vehicle we put him on oxygen and got an IV in, but as soon as we removed him he started to crash.'

'Hypovolaemic shock,' Maggie heard Jake mutter as she stepped aside while the patient was transferred with the backboard and cervical collar still in place.

The young man was certainly showing all the classic signs of severe blood loss.

'Also increasing difficulty in breathing,' the paramedic continued seamlessly. 'There was no sign of a penetrating wound into the chest, so I went with the probability that his lung had been pierced by a broken rib.'

The needle protruding from the midaxillary line of the fourth intercostal space looked surreal under the stark white lighting, especially with a flaccid condom taped to it as a makeshift flutter valve.

'What were his vital signs once his lung reinflated?' Jake demanded as the radiographer positioned the first X-ray cassette under their patient's neck.

'Pulse and breathing both a little rapid, but fear of asphyxia will do that to anyone,' the paramedic added wryly as she handed over the notes that would form part of the patient's case history and collected her equipment. 'My vehicle should be restocked and ready to roll by now. No doubt I'll be seeing you again soon. It's a mess out there.'

'Can somebody find out if there's space in Theatre?' Jake asked urgently, not needing to look up from what he was doing to know that his request would receive immediate attention with a rapid phone call. 'Maggie, get over here quick and get another line in. He needs more blood. It must be more than his lung. If there's no room in Theatre we might have to open his chest down here.'

Almost as if he'd given the cue, several sets of monitoring equipment started sounding out their various warnings even as Maggie started manually pumping another unit of blood.

'He's crashing again!' she exclaimed, reading the

display charting pulse and blood pressure. 'Where's the anaesthetist?' She handed over her task to the nearest pair of willing hands and grabbed the sealed tray thrust towards her. Even as she ripped off the protective cover to reveal the set of sterile equipment, the door swung open to admit the hurrying anaesthetist.

It was like a well-oiled machine. Each of the members of the team performed their part of the job, with items of equipment appearing almost before Jake could ask. With the speed of experience, the chest and upper abdomen were swiftly swabbed to minimise the risk of infection, and after a brief pause for the anaesthetist to nod that the patient was ready Jake was applying the scalpel in a midline incision.

Maggie had suction ready for the moment he opened up the body cavity, but she was horrified by the amount of blood filling the visual field.

'Has the heart been pierced, or is it the aorta?' she asked, her words almost hidden by the continuing sound of suction as she tried to clear enough away for Jake to see what had happened.

'Aorta,' he said succinctly, reaching into the cavity to find out exactly how extensive the damage was. 'Not too bad,' he conceded after a moment. 'Puncture rather than dissection.'

'But bad enough that we're having trouble maintaining enough pressure to keep him alive,' the anaesthetist butted in tersely.

'In other words, get on with it?' Jake challenged without looking away from his task, but Maggie could still see the familiar gleam of determination in his eyes that appeared every time he knew he had a fight on his hands.

Knowing that time was of the essence if the young man was to survive, she could only look on in admiration at the speed with which Jake effected a workable repair, concentrating on stabilising their patient so that he would survive the trip up to Theatre.

'Pressure's better!' the anaesthetist reported. 'Not great, but better.'

In the background, Maggie heard the phone ring.

'That was Liam Blake,' a female voice called a moment later. 'There's a table free in Theatre, if you're ready for it.'

Maggie felt a swift jolt at the unexpected mention of her ex-fiancé's name and a wash of heat over her cheeks at the sudden silence that told her that the rest of her colleagues had suddenly remembered that neither she nor Liam should have been at the hospital. This should have been their wedding day.

'Is he good enough to go?' Jake asked, deferring to the overriding expertise of the man at the head of the table. 'I'd rather not mess about with him any more down here if I can help it, especially with a cardiothoracic surgeon available.'

'A.s.a.p.!' the anaesthetist said with feeling as he systematically disconnected the various leads connecting their patient to the main life-support and monitoring systems, immediately reconnecting them to the portable system that would maintain him until he reached Theatre.

Even as the doors were closing behind him, they were pushed open by the next trolley, with a second following closely behind.

'There isn't going to be time to breathe today,' muttered one of the nurses as she dodged around the paramedic directing the transfer of their next patient, frantically clearing the detritus from the previous one.

'Maggie,' Lina Mackey called from the doorway, beckoning her over with a flustered expression on her usually calm face.

'Problem?' Maggie asked, puzzled to find herself drawn out into the corridor.

'I'm so sorry!' the woman exclaimed, almost wringing her hands. 'I'd completely forgotten that you're getting married today or I'd never have called you in. You should be getting ready for the ceremony…having your hair done or something.'

'It's not a problem,' Maggie soothed, half of her attention on the sudden burst of staccato instructions that told her Jake had another problem patient on his hands. Everything inside her wanted to return to the room to do her part in taking care of the patients. She didn't have the time or the inclination to explain the shambles of her private life when there were more important things to do.

'But…what about your wedding?' Lina demanded. 'This could go on for hours. You could be stuck here—'

'Honestly,' Maggie interrupted, the sound of Jake's muttered curse so clear that she knew the rest of the team must be able to hear every word being said outside the door…they were probably all but falling over in their efforts to hear more clearly. 'It's not a problem, Lina. I can stay as long as I'm needed.'

'But—'

'There isn't going to be a wedding,' she blurted, then had to stifle a groan when a nearby gasp drew her eyes and she recognised the avid gaze of one of the biggest gossips in the whole department.

'Oh, Maggie, I'm so sorry,' Lina said as she patted her arm, but whether it was in support for her cancelled wedding or the fact that her private business would shortly be spread far and wide, Maggie wasn't certain.

'Don't worry about it,' she said with a weak attempt at a smile, and leant her shoulder against the swing door as she backed away from the encounter. 'Just be pleased that I was available to come in today and keep wheeling the patients through.'

Maggie had been prepared to be the focus of at least one pair of eyes when the door slapped shut behind her, but everyone seemed to be concentrating on what they were doing, far too busy to even have noticed that there was a conversation going on outside the room. Then she realised with a wash of embarrassment that there was an almost unearthly silence hanging over a room that would normally have been a babble of orders, requests and the odd quip, and knew that she was the reason.

'I call it true dedication,' Jake muttered, just loudly enough for everyone in the room to hear, even though they were pretending not to listen, 'coming in to work when she could have been jetting off into the sunshine.'

Cancelling the honeymoon was something else she'd completely forgotten to do, Maggie realised, and wondered if she would be able to use today's emergency events as a valid reason to be able to reclaim the cost. If not, perhaps she should just leave this evening as scheduled.

Her primary examination of the patient over, and vital signs recorded, she stepped back behind the screen as a series of X-rays were taken of her next patient and speculated idly that, in the absence of a new husband, she could always ask a handsome Mediterranean waiter to rub sunscreen on the bits she couldn't reach. With nothing and no one to distract her, she might even end up with a decent tan.

At least if she went away she wouldn't have to worry about where she was going to be sleeping to-night, but that still left her with the problem of storing her belongings.

'Fracture at C4, transversely across the vertebral body' was the verdict, even as her hand hovered over the cervical collar, hoping for the all-clear to remove it.

'How bad?' Maggie demanded, suddenly worrying that she might have missed something vital while her thoughts had wandered into her personal life.

'Whatever you do, don't take the collar off,' the radiologist said dryly. 'It's a good job the paramedics know their stuff or we'd probably be looking at pa-ralysis.'

Maggie started breathing again, grateful that her medical faculties had been performing in spite of her-self. With her patient stabilised as far as possible, all she had to do was hand the rest of his treatment over to someone from Orthopaedics…that and renew her resolve to keep her mind on her job.

When the current crisis was over would be soon enough to worry about moving her belongings out of her place and sorting out the rest of her life.

'How are you doing?' Jake murmured some time later, his deep voice breaking into her concentration, startling her when it emerged so close to her and sending a quiver of awareness through her.

Was he asking whether she was coping with the

unrelenting pace of work? He shouldn't, because she was certain she'd more than proved herself capable over the last two years. They'd already had two DOAs since they'd arrived today, and she'd lost count of the other cases who'd come through their hands. And this was just one of the rooms coping with the influx.

Or was he referring to the unspoken rumours surrounding her about the cancelled wedding? She could hardly be oblivious to the mixture of pity and speculation in her colleagues' eyes, or the odd muttered comments that she wasn't supposed to hear. More direct interrogation would probably come as soon as anyone had enough spare breath to ask the first question.

There was one thing she knew he *couldn't* be asking about, not in front of such an avid audience. In fact, the newly discovered coward inside her wondered if there would ever be a time when the two of them could discuss what had happened between them last night.

'I'm fine,' she reassured him brightly, deliberately avoiding meeting those dark blue eyes, certain they would pick up on her confusion.

'Well, I'm not fine,' he announced, and she found herself holding her breath, wondering what on earth was coming next. 'Without offending anyone's sensibilities, I shall merely say that when I was paged to come here this morning I was rudely dragged out of my favourite fantasy, and I didn't even have time for a cup of coffee.'

There was a good-natured round of laughter and agreement about the lack of refreshment and a couple of male hoots about the reference to fantasies.

Maggie hoped she was the only one who saw the sudden heat in his eyes.

CHAPTER THREE

His favourite fantasy?

He'd been joking…hadn't he?

Over the next two hours Maggie found herself stealing surreptitious glances at Jake as he dealt with everything from simple fractures to an insidious internal haemorrhage from a damaged spleen, but there was absolutely no sign that he'd meant what he said.

'Dream on,' she whispered under her breath, granted a moment's respite until her next patient was wheeled in. It might have sounded as if he reciprocated the attraction she'd been battling for the last two years, but the desire she'd thought she'd glimpsed in his eyes must have been nothing more than wishful thinking.

'This is Mrs Sonja Goss,' the young nurse said as she parked a wheelchair beside the freshly sheeted bed. She assisted the shaking woman as she stood and manoeuvred her way onto the higher perch, careful not to jar the large dressing wrapped around one side of her head and face. At least they'd progressed to the patients with the less life-threatening injuries now.

'Hello, Mrs Goss. I'm Maggie—one of the doctors. What have you done to yourself?' She reached out to begin unwrapping the gauze bandage.

'Hit my head when the car crashed,' she whispered painfully, her speech distorted by her attempt not to move her face any more than necessary. 'Felt as if my whole head exploded and my eye…' She gestured weakly, the tremor in her hand mute testimony to her shocked state.

By the time she faded into silence the last of the dressing had been taken away and Maggie didn't need any more details. She could see exactly what had happened.

'I'm going to need X-rays and a maxillofacial consultant in here,' she said over her shoulder, then bent to lift blood-matted blonde hair aside to take a closer look at the damage, knowing that her requests would be dealt with as swiftly as possible.

'What's happened to my face?' A pain-filled grey eye gazed miserably at her. 'How bad is it? Am I going to look…?' She grimaced then caught her breath, clearly regretting the change in expression when it increased her misery.

Maggie's heart went out to her patient, knowing that facial injuries could strike hard, especially in someone who had previously been as beautiful as this woman had. She certainly didn't look anywhere near the thirty-nine years that her notes said she was.

'The tissues have swollen up temporarily as a result of the blow, so I won't be able to tell exactly how bad it is underneath until we take some X-rays,' she hedged.

'Please!' Mrs Goss whispered urgently, her hand hovering protectively several inches away from her face. 'Tell me the truth. What's been damaged and how obvious is it going to be? I need to know.'

Maggie drew the lingering hand away to hold it reassuringly in her own.

'You hit your head hard enough to crack the bone,' she admitted, deliberately not elaborating with the probability that she'd actually shattered the eye-socket.

'What about all the blood? Am I going to be badly scarred?' She broke off to laugh but there was an edge of hysteria in the sound rather than humour. 'God, I can't believe the irony of it,' she said bitterly, turning her face away. 'I was actually on my way to see a plastic surgeon when *this* happened. I don't stand a chance now.'

Before Maggie could ask what she meant, the radiographer and maxillofacial surgeon arrived almost simultaneously and she had to step back to allow them to do their work.

It was nearly half an hour later when she chanced to look across the room and saw that Mrs Goss was still there. She was looking more miserable than ever, and although Maggie knew that what the radiographer had found was bad enough, her patient's despairing words had lingered.

'Still waiting to be taken up to the surgical ward?' she asked as a way of starting the conversation.

'For all the good it will do me,' she said quietly.

For a moment Maggie was at a loss. Only the certainty that the poor woman had a major problem on her mind made her determined to persevere.

'Tell me,' she demanded softly, perching herself on the edge of the bed so that her body formed a screen between the unhappy woman and the rest of the room.

'Tell you what?' Sonja stonewalled, clearly already sinking into depression.

'Do the words "I don't stand a chance, now" and "For all the good it will do me" sound familiar?' Maggie challenged gently. 'Can't you tell me what's going on?'

She was silent for so long that Maggie wondered if she should give up the attempt Sonja Goss hadn't had time to get to know her well enough to trust her with painful confidences. Perhaps one of the staff on the surgical ward would have more chance of getting her to open up about what was preying on her mind.

'Who is he?' Mrs Goss demanded suddenly, pointing to someone over Maggie's shoulder. 'The good-looking one with the dark hair and blue eyes.'

Even without looking, Maggie knew who she meant. It could only be Jake Lascelles.

'You mean the one with the dimples and shoulders and testosterone to spare?' she said teasingly, raising her voice just enough to make sure that he heard her. Jake obliged by throwing a blinding grin their way that brought out both his dimples to best effect—and sent her own hormones quivering.

'He's my boss,' she continued in a normal voice. 'Why did you want to know?'

'Because he looks a bit like my husband—the sort of man who can't help making every woman look at him and wish he was hers.'

'And?' Maggie prompted gently. 'That sounds like a good thing?'

'It would be if he weren't surrounded by bright young things all day, and all he's got to come home to at the end of the day is his middle-aged wife.' She paused to draw a steadying breath and shook her head. 'I'm sorry,' she whispered. 'You don't need to hear all this.'

'Yes, I do, if it's something that's worrying you,' Maggie reassured her, grateful that she actually had a few minutes to spend with the poor woman. If she'd arrived a couple of hours ago, it would have been a very different matter. 'Was that why you were going to see a plastic surgeon?'

Sonja chuckled wryly as she gestured towards her bruised and broken face. 'This lot makes wrinkles and a face-lift seem a bit trivial, doesn't it? I won't even look human any more, let alone—'

'Actually, you might do rather well out of the accident,' Maggie interrupted with a sudden flash of inspiration, shocking her patient into silence. 'Obviously, I'm not a plastic surgeon, but from what I've heard, one way of doing a face-lift is by cutting around the hairline and trimming away the loose skin before stitching everything up again. Is that what you were going to have done?'

'Well, something like that,' Sonja agreed. 'It sounds pretty ghastly when you put it like that.'

'Well, that's roughly what the maxillofacial surgeon will have to do when he rebuilds your eye socket. All you'll have to do is ask him to pull the skin a little tighter and trim off the excess before he stitches everything back again. And as this is England, and the operation's the result of an accident rather than elective surgery, the whole thing won't cost you a penny.'

'You're kidding! Really?' There was a rapidly growing spark of interest in her eyes.

'Your chariot awaits,' Jake announced at that moment, making Maggie nearly jump out of her skin. She'd had no idea he was standing so close.

'Ready to go?' She supported Sonja as she slid carefully to the edge of the bed and gingerly lowered herself into the waiting wheelchair. To her surprise, she felt her hackles rise when she noticed that the woman was giving Jake a thorough inspection—as though one night together gave her any right to feel proprietorial about him.

'He's even better-looking up close,' Sonja murmured suddenly, and in spite of the painkillers deadening sensation in her face and distorting her speech, Maggie knew from her expression that she'd intended him to hear.

'You shouldn't have told him that,' she scolded, playing along. 'He might get a swollen head.'

'Well, I hope there'll still be enough room inside it to make sure he appreciates his junior staff,' she said with a swift return to sincerity. 'If it hadn't been for your patience I would probably be suicidal by now. Instead...' She turned cautiously to look up at him. 'Do you know, she's actually found a way for me to look at this...' she gestured towards the heavily padded side of her face '...as a stroke of luck?'

'All part of the service, ma'am!' Jake quipped with a bow, then stepped aside to allow the porter to set off with the wheelchair.

'Another satisfied customer. Well done,' he murmured, and it wasn't just the quiet words of praise that sent a warm glow spreading through her. In spite of herself, she couldn't help responding to the gleam in his eye that told her that his words meant more than simple approval for a junior colleague's work— or was it that he hadn't forgotten last night either?

'There's not a lot of point going home now,' one of the junior staff nurses groaned as she sank onto the arm of the settee, a steaming cup of coffee clutched in one hand. 'I'd have to turn round and come back in almost as soon as I got there.'

'Me, too,' chorused several others.

'Still, the overtime will come in handy, with Christmas coming,' added another voice, but Maggie wasn't really paying much attention. Now that the emergency was over, she'd suddenly remembered that, apart from getting married, she was supposed to have been moving house today.

'Here,' a voice said. An elbow nudged hers and she looked up into Jake's dark blue eyes. 'Grab this while it's hot,' he ordered, and they juggled for possession of the steaming mug of coffee without burning their fingers.

Suddenly, she had an all too vivid memory of the results of last time they'd shared coffee, and she felt a swift wash of heat travel up her throat and into her face.

'You'll need these, too,' he added quietly, surreptitiously slipping something into her hand.

'What…?'

'You need to move your stuff before the new tenant comes with a lynching party,' he said, making her wonder if he'd taken up mind-reading. How could he know that was what she'd been worrying about just then? 'These are the keys to my flat. You might as well dump everything there until you find something else.'

'I can't impose on you like that,' she objected, even though the offer would solve the problem of where to store her stuff. She tried to give the keys back but he wouldn't accept them.

'You need somewhere to put everything until you find a new place,' he pointed out.

'But I couldn't—'

'I've got a spare room,' he interrupted with a shrug, 'Are you sure?' She tightened her hand around the assortment of keys, using the sharp jabbing of the edges in her palm to bring her thoughts back to earth.

'I'm only sorry I haven't got enough time to help you move. I've rearranged it so that my shift starts in about half an hour. Do you want to borrow my car?'

'No way!' she exclaimed. 'I haven't driven for ages and I'm not starting on that ton-up roller-skate. I'll take a taxi, thank you. I haven't got any furniture to move, so I can probably take everything in one journey. I'd have to do half a dozen in your two-seater.'

'Are you sure you don't want a chance to see how she goes?' he tempted with a boyish grin that showed off those dimples again. 'Your street cred would be sky-high.' He drained the last of his coffee and held his hand out for her mug.

'I'm sure it would, if I were interested in having street cred,' she said soothingly, knowing what a tender plant the male ego was. 'But all I'm interested in is moving my stuff with the minimum of fuss and effort.'

'Please yourself,' he said with a good-natured shrug, and shortened his stride to match hers as they set off along the corridor. 'What do you want for breakfast?'

'Breakfast?' she echoed, confused by the sudden change of topic and once more reminded of the fact that they hadn't even got as far as breakfast together this morning.

'I make mine when I come home at the end of my shift so I might just as well prepare it for two. When we know how long you're staying, we can sort out some sort of rota,' he explained with patient logic.

Except it wasn't logical at all.

'Staying? I won't be staying—'

'Of course you will,' he interrupted briskly. 'None of your friends have got the room to take you, there's no way you're going to find another flat in the next couple of hours, and your salary certainly wouldn't support a lengthy stay in an hotel. It could take days or even weeks.'

His tone completely demolished any lingering suspicion that he might have made the offer in the hope of a repeat of last night's activities. Clearly he preferred the title of good Samaritan to that of Don Juan and it was totally ridiculous to feel disappointed that the thought obviously hadn't crossed his mind. Then his words registered fully.

'Weeks!' She was horrified at the thought. It had been bad enough hiding her attraction from him when they'd lived separate lives, but sharing a flat after they'd shared the ultimate intimacy of making love... 'I can't stay with you that long. You moved into the flat so you could have your own space.'

'Maggie, I wouldn't have offered if I didn't want you there,' he pointed out. 'Now, stop worrying about everything and go and get yourself moved in. I'll see you in the morning.'

Maggie hovered indecisively. One part of her was leaping up and down at the very idea of moving in with Jake, but the other part was definitely feeling guilty. It wasn't his fault that she was homeless, so why should he have to put up with the inconvenience of an unwanted guest?

'On the understanding that it's strictly temporary,' she temporised to salve her conscience, even as she fought down the rising excitement.

'Whatever,' he said dismissively, clearly totally unmoved by the fact that he'd invited her to share his sanctuary. He waved her off. 'Just go and get on with it.'

The sound of Jake's key in the lock sent Maggie's pulse into overload.

With a sudden attack of nerves, she flung herself onto one end of the plush leather sofa, hoping to disguise the fact that she'd been hovering by the door for the last hour. The noisy outbreak of leathery squeaks as the cushions settled around her almost destroyed the effect and had her fighting the urge to giggle.

She watched silently as he leant back against the door, the click as the lock caught echoing round the room like a pistol shot. He toed off his shoes and kicked them into the corner under the coatrack and she followed every move, fascinated by the glimpse of what was obviously a well-worn routine.

She could easily get used to this…getting to know the everyday quirks and foibles that made up his private life…too easily!

A sharp pain wrapped itself around her heart as she reminded herself that this was a purely temporary measure. She was just an unwanted a guest, not a part of Jake's life, no matter how much she'd always wanted to be.

Still, she couldn't help feasting her eyes on him as he slid his jacket off his shoulders, juggling a loaded briefcase and a precarious pile of files as he extricated his arms one at a time.

He turned to hang it on one of the hooks on the wall beside the front door and ploughed into the pile of boxes she'd deposited there.

'Ouch! Dammit!'

'Oh, Jake, I'm sorry!' she exclaimed, and it was only when he whirled in surprise at her voice, dropping his paperwork all over the floor and narrowly missing his foot with his briefcase, that she realised she'd been so fascinated watching him that she'd completely forgotten to let him know she was there.

'Oh, Lord, what a mess!' Maggie fought her way out of the squashy embrace of the settee and hurried across to help him gather up the scattered papers. 'I didn't mean to make you jump.'

'What's that stuff doing there anyway?' he demanded gruffly and her spirits sank even lower.

'Jake... You said I could bring it here, remember? Just until I find—'

'Of course I remember,' he interrupted. 'I'm exhausted, not senile.' He straightened up with the last of the notes he'd taken at the previous departmental meeting clutched in his hand. 'I meant, what's it doing out here when I distinctly remember telling you that you could use my spare room?'

'Oh, well...I didn't really like to go poking around when you weren't here,' she said apologetically. 'I was waiting for you to come back. And, anyway, there's no point in unpacking everything. I'll be moving out as soon as possible.'

He frowned at that, but before he could say anything there was the sound of a timer going off in the kitchen.

'What on earth is that?'

'Supper,' she said succinctly, grateful for the reprieve. She didn't think she would ever win an argument with Jake about the length of time she stayed with him, especially when a large part of her would like nothing better than to settle in permanently.

'Something smells good!' he exclaimed, following his nose towards the archway leading to the kitchen. 'You found the menus for the local take-aways, did you?'

She followed him as far as the wooden-topped counter and watched as he bent to peer through the glass door of the microwave.

'Try the oven,' she suggested when he found it empty.

'You cooked?' Both eyebrows went up.

'Well, there's no need to sound so shocked,' she complained. 'I *can* cook, you know.'

'You haven't had much chance to practise in your recent accommodation, so I'll have to take your word for it. Your skills have probably gone rusty,' he teased, reaching for the oven gloves waiting beside the cooker.

'Be prepared to eat your words.' She whisked the oven gloves out of his hands and opened the door. 'Oh, and you could make yourself useful by opening the bottle of wine on the table.'

'Wine, too? What are we celebrating, and how often does it happen in a year?'

Maggie chuckled as she carried the sizzling dish of lasagne to the table and silently wondered what she'd been worried about as the last of her tension evaporated. This was the Jake she'd worked beside for the last two years, always ready with a teasing quip. Her brother, David, had been like that when they'd been growing up—always able to lighten the atmosphere and make her feel as if she was really part of the family instead of an unnecessary hanger-on.

'It's a combination of an apology and a thank you,' she explained as she cut and served a man-sized portion onto one plate and handed it to Jake. 'Help yourself to salad.'

'Apology for what and thanks for what?' he mumbled around his first steaming bite, then groaned in appreciation. 'Oh, this is fantastic! Why can't you get anything that tastes like this out of a freezer?'

'Because this is what it tastes like when you use fresh ingredients and make it completely from scratch. Packets and tins will never be able to compete with that,' she said smugly.

Silence reigned for several moments, broken only by Jake's theatrical moans of enjoyment, and Maggie was basking in his approval until she realised just how similar they were to the sounds he'd made last night when he'd been savouring some very different flavours...

'So, tell me,' he insisted as he reached out to serve himself a second helping. 'What *did* I do to warrant this bounty?'

'Saved me from sleeping under a railway arch, for a start,' she said as she held the salad bowl towards him. 'I know you moved into this flat so you could have some peace and quiet, so I really appreciate you putting me up like this. I'll try not to get in your way too much, and if you let me know when you want to have visitors, I can always arrange—'

'Stop right there!' he ordered with a scowl. 'Until you find yourself something suitable, all you've got to remember is that you're not here on sufferance. You'd do the same for me if our positions were reversed—that's what friends do for each other—so I don't want to hear another word about it.'

'But—'

'Maggie, don't argue. Don't you realise how hard

this is for me? If I allowed you to grovel regularly, I could have you cooking meals like this for ever, so please allow me my moment of self-sacrifice.'

'Idiot!' she spluttered around a mouthful of wine, almost choking at his nonsense. 'I'd be perfectly happy to cook for you if I'm first home.'

'OK, then. That's how we'll play it,' he announced. 'First one home can start the cooking and the other one gets clean-up duty.'

'That sounds a lot fairer than my brother's system.' She chuckled. 'He was always organising me—usually into doing the chores he hated!'

'Before you think you've got a good deal, wait till you see how many times I can wangle coming home last just so you get to do the cooking.'

When they'd finished eating, Jake tried to persuade her to let him clean up, but she'd been enjoying their conversation so much that it was no trouble to dry the dishes and put them away while they discussed the traumatic events at the hospital that day.

'Time for bed!' he announced, when she yawned for the second time and she nearly swallowed her tongue.

'Wh-what?' she gasped and could have murdered him on the spot when he laughed.

'Don't get me wrong about this,' he continued, apparently seriously. 'It's not that I didn't enjoy myself last night, but after the day we've had I really don't think I'm up to a repeat performance. So, if you don't mind, I'll show you to the spare room and find you some clean sheets for the bed.'

An hour later, Jake wasn't feeling so much like laughing.

He was absolutely exhausted, after a night with

very little sleep followed by a day from hell in the accident and emergency department, but his brain just wouldn't shut down.

It had been difficult to switch off his thoughts before, when he'd been living in the room next door to Maggie and had been able to hear the everyday sounds she made. This was far worse. Now it wasn't just his imagination that insisted on playing images of her slender arms welcoming him into her bed and her body—he had the memories, too.

Memories of the flesh-and-blood woman revealed to him when her sodden dressing-gown had plummeted to the floor of the shower cubicle with a resounding splat.

'Oh, Maggie,' he groaned when he remembered how tightly furled her nipples had been under the onslaught of the cold water, and the way the rivulets had chased each other over every curve and hollow.

He'd been so busy gazing at those curves and hollows that he'd barely been aware of her trembling hands fighting to undo his shirt buttons until she'd whimpered her frustration.

'I want to see you, too,' she'd said, and the words had nearly brought him to his knees. It wasn't much better now, in spite of the fact that his two-year drought had been broken in spectacular fashion last night. If his body wasn't exhausted, it should at least have lost some of the sense of urgency that had gripped him when he'd realised what Maggie wanted.

Oh, he'd tried to be noble…briefly…but her only response had been to reach for his head with both hands, sliding her fingers through his hair to pull him closer.

'If you don't want to make love with me, then say so,' she'd said, her steady words totally at odds with her trembling body and the heart-stopping vulnerability in those stunning blue-green eyes.

He'd had to look away in case she'd seen just how *much* he'd wanted to. He'd never wanted anything more.

He'd been certain that he could do the right thing until she'd whispered, 'I need you!' The pleading in her voice had been something he'd never thought he'd hear from the Maggie he'd known for the last two years. Then she'd reached for the fastening of his waistband and his resolution to practice noble restraint had disappeared completely.

He'd never forget the way she'd fitted in his arms, that first contact so perfect that he'd nearly lost control like an untried adolescent. She was so slender and lithe that the full curves of her breasts had been unexpected...and far more of a temptation than he could resist. All he'd been able to think of was touching and tasting, possessing and being possessed, and he'd willingly given in to her body's demands, all attempts at finesse forgotten in their meteoric ascent into ecstasy.

'Wow! What do you do for an encore?' she'd said with a chuckle, and his heart had soared with the implied compliment. He'd been certain that exhaustion would prevent any repeat, until she'd tightened those intimate muscles around him where he'd still been buried deep inside her and had proved him wrong.

She'd laughed again, a throaty, husky laugh that had detonated a bolt of arousal through his nervous system, exploding all his previous conceptions of his physical capabilities.

'Enough!' he groaned, muffling the sound in his pillow. He needed sleep, not endless replays of the most spectacular night of his life. Anyway, there was no point in going over every last caress like a lover looking forward to the next time they could be together, thinking of ways to heighten their pleasure still further. It wasn't going to happen.

His night with Maggie had been a once-in-a-lifetime event, and the sooner his body and his brain got the message, the better. She might have needed him last night, in the wake of the evening's disastrous events, but there was no way he could ever be a permanent part of her life. There could never be anything more than friendship between them because he could never be what she wanted. He had decided long ago that he was going to build his life around his career, and nothing was going to change that decision.

CHAPTER FOUR

'HEY, Jake! Glad to see you. We need you in here, pronto!' the anaesthetist called, and in spite of the fact that her brain and hands were working at full speed on her latest patient, Maggie's heart gave that newly familiar skip before settling into a faster rhythm.

When was it going to settle down again? she thought crossly, bending her head over her patient as she fought to stem the blood jetting out of the all but severed brachial artery.

While one part of her mind was calculating how long the injured cyclist could afford to lose blood at this rate before succumbing to cardiac failure, the other part was totting up the number of days—nearly three weeks so far—that had elapsed since *that night*.

'What's going on in here, then?' Jake demanded, already donning gloves as he approached the table. 'What have we got?'

'Cyclist versus high-speed car,' Maggie said shortly. She'd lost count of the number of staff currently battling to save the youngster's life. There was almost no space left in the room, with everybody intently focused on their specific task, and still the outcome was doubtful. 'I think I've got the shredded brachial artery under control. Could you check the femoral? The bone's a mess and might have compromised it.'

'He's leaking like a sieve,' Jake muttered after an all-encompassing glance at the patient's multitude of injuries as he positioned himself on the other side of the table. He immediately began investigating yet another probable source of blood loss, this time hidden within the patient's misshapen thigh. 'Tell me you've got more blood on the way.'

'I think we need it delivered by the bucket to keep up with this rate of loss,' Maggie muttered, feeling unaccountably queasy at the sight of so much gore.

That was something totally unexpected. She'd barely turned a hair right from the earliest days of her training, so developing a sensitivity to the sight and smell of it after all this time was ridiculous.

Suddenly her ears were assaulted by several warnings going off at once, terminating in the steady tone that told of a flat line on the heart monitor.

'Dammit! He's arrested!' Jake swore. He reached out automatically to begin chest compressions then, before Maggie could say anything, abandoned the attempt without laying a hand on the bloodied body. 'Too many broken ribs,' he said in disgust. 'I'll have to open his chest.'

'I don't know if it's worth the effort,' the neurologist said grimly, indicating the X-ray of the skull. 'The bone is completely shattered right across the back of his head and the fragments have been driven right into his brain stem. I don't know if they make scores low enough on the Glasgow coma scale for what's happened to this poor kid.'

For a moment there was silence while everyone looked from their patient to Jake and back, waiting for the inevitable decision. With that level of damage to the all-important brain stem they all knew that any hope of recovery was gone, even if they could restart his heart, but Maggie could see that it went against everything she knew about Jake to admit defeat. Then his shoulders slumped and he shook his head, silently admitting the futility of doing any more.

'Time of death?' he demanded gruffly, glancing up at the inexorably ticking clock, and nodded his agreement when it was called out and added to the case notes.

'A sad end to Damian Fisher's life,' Maggie said softly as she joined him to deposit her blood-stained gloves and apron. 'Someone must have been travelling far too fast to do that much damage.'

'Not necessarily, but all too often that's the case,' Jake agreed sombrely as he shouldered the swing door open for her then followed her out into the corridor. She heard him sigh wearily and a sideways glance told her that the dark circles under his eyes didn't look any better than they had the day before. They could be caused by his stressful job, but he'd always seemed to cope before. Was he having as much difficulty sleeping as she was? Were his dreams as full of heated memories as…?

'Coffee?' she suggested, determined not to go down that path with the man who starred in those night-time fantasies only inches away. 'Do you think we'll have time to drink it before the relatives arrive?' She wouldn't let herself imagine what panic that phone call would have set in motion, and this time there could be no happy outcome.

'We can but try.' Jake sounded unhappy, but Maggie knew it wasn't about the possibility of yet another abandoned cup of coffee. The prospect of telling parents that their bright, healthy son would never grow up to have sons of his own was enough to depress anyone.

The conversation was one that they'd had innu merable times over the last two years, so why did she feel so much more aware of his emotions? Why did she long to find some way of easing the burden for him? Why did even a simple coffee-break feel as if it was something more than two colleagues sharing a brief break in a busy day?

She was being stupid, that was why.

She'd been sharing his flat for weeks, and not by the slightest twitch had Jake indicated that he regret ted what had happened between them, or that he wanted it to happen again. She needed to get her head together or he would soon pick up on the escalation of her feelings towards him—her unwanted feelings towards him. With Jake happy to have her as nothing more than a friend, that could make life so unbearable that she'd have to consider moving to another hos pital, and then she'd never see him at all.

'I wonder how the driver will live with himself when he finds out what he's done,' she commented, needing to focus her attention on something other than the fact that she could smell a lingering hint of Jake's shampoo when they were this close. 'Was the man injured?'

'If he's the one who was being wheeled in as I joined you with Damian, it looked as if he'd hit his head. Probably suffered nothing more than a brief loss of consciousness and will need half a dozen stitches.' He reached out to push open the staff lounge door. 'Sometimes you wonder at the justice of it...'

'No-oo...!'

Jake's final words were almost lost under the howl of despair that echoed around the department. Auto matically they both altered their direction, making for the location of the disturbance. There were far too many incidents of A and E staff being attacked by patients crazy with drink or drugs for any of them to ignore such a sound.

'No! It's not true!' the man was shouting, with equal measures of anger and despair. 'You're lying!'

'What's going on in here?' Jake demanded, the weight of authority in his voice and bearing.

For a moment his voice made everyone freeze into a strange tableau, and it made Maggie think of a childhood game of Statues.

There was the patient, one side of his face streaked with the blood still trickling from the ugly gash at his temple, and a white-faced nurse beside him looking as if she'd rather be anywhere else. The rest of the staff had strange expressions on their faces...the closest Maggie could come was to call it horrified fascination.

'This nurse is lying to me,' the man shouted, first to recover from Jake's arrival. 'She said my son's been brought into hospital. She said he's been hit by a car...that I hit my own son!'

Maggie felt sick. Of all the scenarios she could have imagined, this would have been the last.

'What is your son's name?' Jake asked calmly, logical as ever.

'Fisher. Damian Fisher. And he doesn't even own a bike. I won't let him have one because they're too bloody dangerous,' he announced, then added belligerently, 'Now, you'd better apologise, or I'll be making a complaint to the hospital authorities. In fact, I think I'll make one anyway—'

'Mr Fisher,' Jake interrupted quietly, and the mere tone of his voice silenced the bad-tempered bluster.

'This isn't the way I would have liked to break bad news to anybody, but your son *was* brought into hospital today and he *had* been knocked down by a car.'

'Oh, my God,' Mr Fisher breathed, his eyes going wide with shocked comprehension. 'Not Damian! He's going to be all right, isn't he? He's not badly hurt?' He began to scramble off the table, oblivious of his state of dress. 'Can I see him? I *must* see him. Where is he?'

'Of course you can see him,' Jake agreed, catching him by the elbow as the man staggered with the combination of his own injuries and disbelief at the news he'd been given, his face even paler than before. 'Please, sit down for a moment. You're in shock.'

'Of course I'm in bloody shock, man! I've just heard my son's hurt.' He didn't have the strength to fight Jake and subsided weakly onto the edge of the table. 'Tell me how he is.'

'Unfortunately, he was badly injured,' Jake began gently, using a familiar format that made Maggie feel inadequate every time she had to use it herself. 'We did everything we could, but—'

'What do you mean—*you did everything you could*?' he demanded, too impatient to wait for Jake to finish. 'What's wrong with my son? What have you done with him?'

'Unfortunately, his injuries were too severe and there was nothing we could do to save him.'

'What? *No!* It's not true! It *can't* be true!' The denials were painful to hear and even more painful to watch as the full realisation dawned on him that he'd killed his own son.

Even as Maggie watched, the man began to tremble all over, his face turning a cold waxen grey.

'Watch him,' she muttered to Jake, her antennae warning her of impending trouble. 'He's going to go.'

Even as she was speaking, Mr Fisher groaned and slumped forward, one arm hanging heavily as he clutched his chest with the other.

'Dammit!' Jake swore as he narrowly saved the man from landing on the floor. 'Get him back on the table and get some leads on him. I need to know what's happening in his heart *now*!'

'What a day!' Jake groaned. He leaned back against the door and heard the lock catch with a satisfying click, shutting the world out for a while. Here, in his own little domain, he was secluded enough to unwind and recharge his batteries ready for—

'Did you hear whether Mr Fisher made it?'

The sound of Maggie's voice reaching him from the darkness still shocked him. Over the last couple of years he'd grown so accustomed to switching off the fanciful imaginings of coming home to find her waiting for him that he sometimes forgot that she was really here.

'What are you doing, sitting in the dark?' He reached for the light switch, using the dimmer function so that he didn't blind her with the sudden glare.

'I wasn't actually sitting,' she admitted sheepishly as her head appeared over the back of the settee.

His heart gave an extra thump at the sight of her. Ever since they'd met he'd had a weakness for toffee-coloured hair and eyes that could never decide whether they were green or blue.

'I was only going to sit down for a minute when I came in,' she continued round a yawn, 'and I just sort of fell asleep.'

She hardly needed to tell him. Her hair was endearingly tousled and her eyes still looked drowsy, just the way he'd imagined them a thousand times. But in his mind it hadn't been sleep that made her look that way.

'So... Mr Fisher...?' she prompted with a frown, and he realised he'd gone off into a world of his own for a moment, a world he couldn't afford to visit at all while she was under his roof. It was bad enough that he'd taken advantage of her distress when she'd had to call off her wedding. It would be unconscionable to do the same while she was taking refuge...

'Oh, Mr Fisher.' He paused to clear the huskiness from his voice and gather his thoughts. 'He's holding his own so far, but they're issuing the usual warning about surviving the first twenty-four hours.'

'Thank God for that,' Maggie said softly. 'I don't know if his wife would have coped with losing her whole family on the same day. She was already pretty hysterical when she arrived in A and E to find out what had happened to her son, then to discover that her husband was being resuscitated after going into cardiac arrest...'

'The stuff nightmares are made of,' he agreed, and made his way towards the kitchen, automatically draping his jacket over the arm of the chair as he went past then beginning to roll up his sleeves. 'Sorry I'm so late when it's my turn to cook. I haven't a clue what's in the cupboard.'

'I took the lasagne out of the freezer to defrost.' Her voice floated in from the other room. 'It shouldn't need much more than nuking in the microwave.'

'Good idea. I know there's some salad stuff in the fridge to go with it.' His taste-buds were already cheering at the thought of more of Maggie's home-made lasagne. She'd made a double batch the other day and told him to freeze half for just such an eventuality.

'Of course we'll need to go into arbitration about this,' she said, her sleep-husky voice so much closer that he knew she'd come to lean in the doorway to watch him. Suddenly he was all thumbs, and in danger of slicing off a fingertip or two if he didn't concentrate on what he was doing rather than the scent of warm woman.

'Arbitration? Over what?' He chopped raw carrot into neat chunks with a satisfying series of thwacks.

'Over whether this counts as a meal *I've* prepared—in which case you now owe me three,' she said with a cheeky grin, then had to move swiftly to catch the piece of carrot he flipped straight at her.

This is how it could have been, she thought with an ache in her heart when they sat down to eat a short while later. If Jake had been the marrying kind... If he had felt the same attraction towards her...

Well, that wasn't strictly accurate. He obviously felt *something* towards her, or they wouldn't have spent the night together, but that wasn't what she was thinking about. What she meant was that he didn't want the same 'for ever after' commitment that she was looking for.

Ah, well. She sighed. She'd better enjoy the light-hearted banter and the fulfilment she got from preparing a meal for him while she could. This might be as close as she got to her dream, and if she only had the courage to seduce the man again...

'That was a heavy sigh,' Jake commented, and she felt a blush begin to heat her cheeks.

Thank goodness he couldn't read her mind, she thought as she frantically hunted for a suitable topic.

'Just tired,' she settled on, all too truthfully. 'And I'm on early again tomorrow, so it isn't going to get any better.'

'You're right,' he agreed as he began to gather their plates. 'Sometimes it seems as if there's hardly enough time to breathe, let alone relax and recuperate at the end of the day.'

'And even then *you* can't relax properly because you're having to put up with a squatter,' she pointed out guiltily. Here she was revelling in the fact that she was able to spend this time with him while he was probably longing to get rid of her. 'I'm sorry, but it's been several days since I had time to contact the letting agencies during office hours, and there just doesn't seem to be anything going at the moment. Not even a dog kennel.'

'Maggie, it's not a problem,' he soothed. 'I've got the spare room and you're more than pulling your weight around the place so—'

'That's not the point!' she interrupted. 'You moved out of the other place so you could have a bit more privacy, and you've ended up with less.'

'Hey, Maggie, calm down. It's not a big problem. I haven't been this well fed since I lived at home, and as for privacy...' He shrugged. 'Don't forget, I had to put up with far worse than this when I was at boarding school. We were five to a room until we got to be seniors. Sharing a spacious flat like this is sheer luxury by comparison.'

'But—'

'Listen, if you're that worried about it, you could

always take over the laundry and Hoovering...and cleaning the bathroom.'

'In your dreams!' She threw a damp tea-towel at his head, surprised to find that they'd finished the washing up while they were talking. 'What did your last slave die of?'

She could tell from the gleam in his eyes that she wouldn't like his suggestion and hastily headed him off.

'Anyway, I shouldn't be in your way for too much longer. I'm hoping to have a look at a place at the weekend—it's a flat-share not far from the place I was living before.'

'What's it like? Who would you be sharing with?'

'Hospital staff again. Apparently, one is the new cardiothoracic registrar,' she said with a grimace, not exactly keen to share with someone working so closely with Liam.

'Couldn't that get a bit uncomfortable?'

'All too easily,' she agreed. 'But I need to find something soon. I can't mooch off you for ever.'

'I'm not complaining,' Jake pointed out blandly. 'In fact, I'd rather you stayed longer and found something you're really happy with than rush into something just for the sake of going.'

Jake knew just how strong Maggie's sense of fairness was. She would have argued herself blue in the face if he hadn't changed the topic of conversation, sidetracking her onto the recently proposed change of shift patterns.

'Idiot!' he muttered half-heartedly into the darkness, once more condemned to a sleepless night. But he didn't really regret persuading her to stay longer.

The discomfort involved in sharing his flat with a woman who could rev his pulse from nought to a thousand with nothing more than the scent of her shampoo was completely outweighed by the pleasure of her presence.

The trouble was, he was in a cleft stick. One part of him wanted to help her in her search, to make sure that she found somewhere nice to live. The other part was only too aware that the more he helped her, the sooner she would leave him.

And every time he closed his eyes he was treated to yet another replay of *that* night, so it didn't much matter whether she was here or not. Awake or asleep, she filled his thoughts and his imagination.

Thank goodness he had a job that also filled his mind. At least when he was faced with the sort of multiple traumas that a high-speed traffic accident produced, his brain did what it had been trained to do. All he had to do was concentrate on getting enough sleep so that his brain would function...

It was still dark when he heard Maggie going to the bathroom early the next morning.

Guiltily, he waited to hear the water start to flow, anticipating the vivid memories of the first time he'd ever seen her naked body. Instead, all too clearly through the confines of the flat, he heard the unmistakable sound of someone being violently sick.

Without any recollection of moving, he found himself standing outside the bathroom door with a glass of water in his hand.

'Maggie?' he called, surprised at just how hard it was to force himself to wait for a reply when everything in him wanted to charge in to see what was wrong with her.

'What?' she snapped, and he couldn't help grinning when he remembered that she absolutely hated being ill. She'd told him that the very idea of a hangover was enough to prevent her from drinking more than her limit.

'Can I come in?' That was another thing she hated—having anyone witness her body letting her down by succumbing to illness.

'Why?' He'd had to wait a moment for that, wincing at the sound of the latest onslaught.

'I've got a glass of cold water and a clean face-cloth,' he offered.

'OK,' she conceded on a groan, but he was already pushing the door open.

His first sight of her aroused all his protective instincts. He didn't think he'd ever seen her looking so pale and fragile, huddled in a crumpled heap on the floor in front of the toilet.

'Here.' He held out the glass to her, but when he saw the way her hand was shaking, he opted for kneeling down beside her and holding it to her lips. 'Take a mouthful to rinse out first, then take a small sip to swallow.'

She threw him a wordless glare of injured pride that he should think she needed instruction, but complied.

The first sip came straight back, but a couple of minutes later she was more successful.

Jake ran the tap till the warm water came through and wrung the facecloth out under the stream.

'Here,' he offered. 'Give your face a wipe. It'll make you feel better.'

He waited until she'd finished then helped her to her feet.

'What would make me feel better is knowing why you aren't being sick, too,' she grumbled. 'We both ate the same meal last night.'

'Then it can't have been the food,' he said logically, relief coursing through him that she was already starting to fight back. She was already looking less waxen and fragile. 'It could be something you caught from one of the patients. We don't always work on the same ones after all.'

'True.' She drew in a careful breath, as though testing to see whether everything was now working properly. 'Well, whatever it is, I don't feel quite so grim now, so I might as well start getting ready for work. There's no point going back to bed.'

She looked up at him expectantly, and for a moment he didn't register that it was an implied request to leave the bathroom. He was far too busy imagining just how much point there would be in going back to bed for an extra half an hour with Maggie. Then he registered the effect such thoughts were having on his body and how obvious that effect would be, given the fact that he was wearing nothing more than a pair of boxer shorts.

'I'll leave you to it, then,' he muttered, hastily turning his back on her to hide the evidence of his desire. 'I'll get the coffee started.'

But it was going to take more than a high-octane cup of coffee to clear his mind of the images of a deliciously naked Maggie massaging shampoo into that tumble of toffee-coloured hair or spreading soap over every sleek dip and hollow.

'Enough!' he groaned, dropping his head forward

against the solid wood of the cabinet door with a hollow thud and leaving it there, hoping that the cool solidity of it would cool the temperature of his thoughts. He was going to have to get his act together in a hurry or she was going to realise there was something wrong.

After her problems with Liam, Maggie didn't need any more stress, least of all her boss lusting after her. In fact, if she made a complaint about him, accused him of sexual harassment, he could lose his job.

That thought was sobering enough to concentrate his mind. After all, his career was all he had.

Suddenly, the prospect of sitting in the same room eating breakfast and breathing in the fresh soapy scent of her hair and skin was unbearable. With a burst of activity he set out juice and coffee and left her to choose whether she had cereal, toast or both.

After dressing, he had his hand on the door when he heard Maggie turn the water off, and he threw one last longing look at the waiting spread, then left for the hospital before he could give in to the desire to wait for her to emerge from the bathroom.

Never mind sharing a leisurely breakfast. What he needed to get his head on straight was a gallon of hospital coffee and a very cold shower.

'What's next on the agenda?' Maggie demanded as she gazed up at the whiteboard, looking for any recent additions written in red.

After triage, the patients' names were put up on the list, the colour of the marker pen denoting the severity of their condition.

'No new reds,' the triage nurse confirmed. 'It's all gone blissfully quiet on the emergency front, and that means you can take your pick between cleaning up a ragged gash and putting in a dozen or so stitches or investigating a badly infected piercing of a—' Her cheerful words were interrupted by the shrill ring of the phone connecting the department directly to Ambulance Headquarters.

'You and your big mouth!' Maggie teased as the crestfallen woman reached for the receiver.

'Accident and Emergency,' she announced crisply, her free hand already extracting a pen from her pocket, ready to take notes. 'What have you got for us?'

Maggie didn't need to be able to hear the other end of the conversation to know that there was something nasty on the way in. Her pulse rose with the resulting surge of adrenaline, readying her for the task ahead.

Almost before she'd put the phone down she was turning to give Maggie the bad news.

'Two motor vehicles rolled over at speed. Possibly eight victims—they'll confirm numbers later. First victims should be with us in ten minutes—assorted breaks, cuts and concussions. Some of the others are trapped and will have to be cut out. Updates later, as and when.'

Almost without another word being said, staff began to hurry to their assigned tasks, preparing the department for the expected influx.

'Ladies and gentlemen.' Maggie's heart gave an extra leap as Jake's voice addressed the waiting patients. 'There has been a traffic accident and we will be receiving several seriously injured patients in the next few hours. This means that those of you with less serious conditions will have to wait longer before there will be anyone free to treat you. I would suggest that if you have a condition that could easily be treated by your GP, it would probably be in your best interests to leave. If you have any further questions, or need advice, have a word with the staff at Reception. Thank you for your patience.'

'From Jake's lips to God's ears,' The anaesthetist muttered. 'Any bets on how long their patience will last?'

Maggie chuckled wryly. 'What was it last time? Two minutes?'

Almost as she spoke there was the sound of raised voices, and she was glad she wasn't anywhere in the vicinity of the reception desk.

'I've been waiting over an hour already!' shouted an unseen man. 'This is disgraceful! I shall be writing to my MP!'

'Any bets on what *he's* here for?' the anaesthetist chimed in irrepressibly. 'I reckon it's an ingrown toenail that's been there for the last twenty years. He sounds like the type.'

Maggie threw him a chiding look, but she knew just how important such off-beat humour was in their fraught jobs. Sometimes, when their working lives got particularly brutal, it was the only thing that kept them grounded in some sort of normality.

Then there was the sound of sirens, and all that mattered was forming up into their teams to receive each patient in turn.

CHAPTER FIVE

'THIS is Garry Wellard, seventeen years old, back-seat passenger without a seat belt,' reported the paramedic accompanying their first patient.

Although his remark could have sounded like a commentary on the stupidity of neglecting simple safety precautions, Maggie knew it was simply a warning of the possible injuries their patient could have sustained.

Accordingly, as he would have hit every surface inside the car when it had rolled over, the young man's neck had been immobilised in a cervical collar and he was strapped to a backboard.

'Obs are surprisingly normal, considering the state of him.'

Maggie was as surprised as the paramedic. There was an inordinate amount of blood splattered all over the youngster, as well as streaming down one side of his face. On that evidence alone she would have expected his blood pressure to be down and his pulse to be fast and thready as his heart revved up to circulate the remaining blood volume to the essential organs.

'Pupils are equal and reactive,' he continued as his patient was being transferred carefully from the trolley onto the table. 'Query Colles' fracture of right wrist, so he must have done a handstand at some stage. Other than that...' He shrugged as he handed over the notes that would form the initial part of the patient's case file. 'I don't know how, but it looks like he's one of the lucky ones.'

Moving with the precision of a well-oiled machine, all seven members of the team closed around the youngster and set to their tasks, examining him from head to toe, taking blood samples for matching, but most importantly cutting away his clothing so that they could get a better look at where all the blood was coming from.

'Hey! Watch what you're doing to my clothes!' the youngster shouted, starting to bat away the nurse with the heavy-duty scissors until he used the wrong hand and jarred his wrist. 'Ow! Leave off! This is my best gear!'

Maggie leaned over him so that the head restriction didn't prevent their eyes meeting.

'So, Garry, you want to be buried in them, do you?' she asked flatly, all too aware that they didn't have any time for niceties. While he was complaining about his clothes being destroyed, he could be bleeding to death from his injuries, external and internal.

'Buried?' He was seventeen, but shock had his voice squeaking into falsetto like a young boy. 'What're you talking about? I'm not dying…am I?'

'We can't tell if we can't examine you,' she pointed out, gesturing to the nurse to continue. The radiographer was already waiting to begin her task of ruling out a potentially fatal broken neck or a lifetime's disability from a broken back. 'You wouldn't expect a garage to try to fix a car without being able to look at the engine, would you?'

Garry grumbled about the waste of money, but subsided enough to let them get on with their tasks.

Fifteen minutes later they were all breathing sighs of relief when they saw the results of the X-rays.

'So that's one head laceration to stitch and one wrist to cast. Otherwise not a mark on him,' the anaesthetist tallied, sounding almost disappointed. 'The blood obviously came from someone else.' The pager at his waist shrilled its summons and he sketched a farewell.

'No doubt we'll find out who at some stage, when they arrive in here,' one of the nurses said.

That wasn't necessarily true, Maggie thought, remembering just how much blood there had been. If someone else in the car with Garry had lost that much volume that soon after the accident, what were the chances that that person had survived this long? It was a depressing fact that they might only see whoever it was for long enough to certify death before they had another patient to deal with.

'Can you believe it? The stupid fools were having a race!' one of the junior sisters was saying as Maggie finally found a free minute to grab something hot to drink.

'In the middle of town?' her friend demanded.

'From a standing start at the traffic lights apparently,' one of the newest registrars detailed with a mixture of fascination and horror. 'The police estimated they were doing a hundred miles an hour and still accelerating when somebody jumped the next set of lights at the crossroads. They tried to take evasive action but were going so fast that one of them flipped and took the other one with it.'

'What was the final tally on death and destruction?'

Maggie asked as she wrapped her hands around the steaming mug.

Not that she needed the heat—that was one thing the hospital never stinted on. If anything the department was kept far too warm for comfort for anyone fully clothed, hence the increasing use of theatre scrubs by staff. No, she was savouring the warmth as a form of comfort during a lull in a particularly gruelling shift.

'Two dead so far,' the young registrar listed grimly. 'There are three in Theatre as we speak, one having his leg amputated in a last-ditch attempt to try to save his life.'

Maggie winced. That was the one that she had worked on in a frantic attempt to stabilise the fourteen-year-old long enough to get him up to Theatre. Although under-age, he'd been the driver in Garry Wellard's car and the one who'd lost all the blood. In spite of her best efforts she didn't hold out much hope for his survival either.

'There's one with a depressed skull fracture and all the signs of brain damage—' he continued his grisly inventory '—and there were a multitude of assorted breaks and lacerations from a femur to a finger, mostly not life-threatening.'

'And the worst thing is that none of it will stop their friends from doing exactly the same thing,' Lina Mackey finished for him in deep disgust. 'Why do these kids not respect life a little more?'

'Because they think they're immortal?' Jake suggested soberly from his position by the darkened window, his hips perched on the convenient window-sill. 'At their age, even getting to twenty seems to be something in the distant future. Life is something to be lived to the full—preferably at a hundred miles an hour—not something to be savoured and revered. I think they just can't believe that anything bad is going to happen to them.'

'I think you're right,' Lina agreed as she rinsed out her cup and placed it upside down on the drainer in her usual tidy way. 'Unfortunately, all the safety campaigns in the world won't put old heads on young shoulders, so we'll continue to try to patch up their shattered bodies and equally shattered lives.'

'On that depressing note, I think I'll go back out into the trenches and see if I can clear a few names off the board,' Maggie said, suddenly not as thirsty as she'd thought.

It wasn't just the tone of the conversation that had spoiled her appetite but the way Jake was ignoring her.

She'd thought she was imagining it, certain that he must have been called in early when he hadn't been there to eat breakfast with her when she'd emerged from the bathroom that morning. But ever since she'd arrived for her shift, he'd seemed to have been at great pains to avoid her company as much as possible.

For the last two years, if they'd managed to take a break at the same time, he'd always come across to take the seat beside her or, failing that, perch on the arm of her chair or lean against the nearest solid surface so that they could talk easily.

Today he wasn't even looking in her direction, and although she'd racked her brains, she couldn't think of anything she'd done to upset him—apart from squatting in his spare room, her conscience reminded her. But just last night he'd told her that it wasn't a problem, so what was she to believe?

A sudden burst of laughter dragged her back to the conversation, wondering who or what had managed to lighten the atmosphere.

'What did I miss?' she asked her closest neighbour.

'It was that paramedic again,' the nurse said through her chuckles. 'Apparently, that's the third time recently that she's used a condom as a flutter valve for a pneumothorax, and the male members of staff...' she glared pointedly across at the new young registrar '...were wondering if she was doing it to attract their attention. You know, letting them know she's always got some on hand in an emergency.'

The registrar's cheekbones darkened and Maggie felt a brief pang when she recognised the opening salvoes in another battle of the sexes. How long would it be before these two realised the significance of their sniping as a symptom of their attraction towards each other and did something about it? Or would they, too, be doomed to eternal friendship?

On that return to depression, she knew it was time to get out of her chair and get going. Keeping busy was probably the best solution. If she kept her brain too full of work to allow random thoughts to intrude...

But even while she was thinking that something was nagging incessantly at the back of her mind... something that someone had said that she should have taken notice of...something important...something that...

Condoms!

She sat down again with a thud, her legs completely refusing to hold her weight as the shock hit her.

Dear God, they hadn't used condoms!

Suddenly everything came together, all the niggling little symptoms she'd been noticing over the last few days, culminating in the spectacular arrival of sickness this morning.

Was she pregnant? Could she be, after just one night?

That was stupid. Of course she could be. Doctors' surgeries all over the world were filled with women convinced it couldn't happen to them...

'Maggie?' There was concern in Jake's voice, and a tone that told her it wasn't the first time he'd tried to attract her attention.

Suddenly she realised that she must have been staring at him across the room. What had he seen in her expression? Horror that she'd just discovered what a fool she'd been not to think about protection until weeks after the event? Or a dawning delight at the very idea that she might be pregnant with his baby?

Might be. Those were the operative words, she counselled herself when all she wanted to do was jump to her feet and execute a manic dance of joy.

After all, she was leaping to conclusions. She might be completely wrong, so the first thing she had to do before she breathed a word to Jake was administer a test.

'Maggie? What's the matter?' He was actually making his way across the room towards her now, and she really didn't think she could stand being that close to him until she had her answer.

'Nothing, Jake. I'm fine,' she squeaked as she shot out of her chair, almost knocking him over in her hurry to get away. 'I just remembered something I forgot to do...' She abandoned the attempt at con-

versation and, rude though it was, tore out of the room
like a cat with her tail on fire.

It was the work of precious few minutes to get her
hands on one of the one-step pregnancy testing kits
and shut herself in the toilet, but it took a lot longer
after the tell-tale line appeared before she was composed enough to unlock the door again.

'*I'm pregnant!*' she whispered to her reflection as
she held her wrists under the cold tap, hoping it would
help to calm her down.

She still didn't know whether shock or delight was
going to win the battle because she was feeling equal
quantities of both.

The more she thought about it, the more obvious it
should have been, considering she'd been hoping to
come back from her honeymoon pregnant. She'd already calculated that it would have been the optimum
time in her cycle, and there had been no need for her
to think about contraception when she'd believed that
Liam had been every bit as eager to have a child as
she was.

No! She wasn't going to think about that. It was
all in the past and had nothing to do with the miracle
already happening inside her.

She pressed a trembling hand against herself, un-
caring of the wet handprint she would leave on the
baggy cotton top, and marvelled.

Deep inside, the fusion of male sperm with female
ovum was growing by the hour, the cells dividing and
multiplying in the initial predestined stages that
would produce a totally unique individual—the child
that she and Jake had made.

Was it a girl or a boy? Would it have his dark hair

and deep blue eyes or her toffee coloured curls and greeny-blue eyes or a mixture of both?

She smiled, already imagining a little boy with a cheeky grin running after a ball, then a curly-headed girl with Jake's determined expression on her face as she urged her pony to go faster.

Her feet barely felt as if they were touching the ground as she floated out of the bathroom...and ploughed straight into Jake outside the door.

'Maggie, are you sure you're all right?' he demanded seriously. 'Have you got some sort of bug?'

She couldn't help the wide smile that took over her face at the evidence that he still cared about her. If they weren't so desperately busy, she could have taken him to one side and given him the news straight away.

'Jake, I'm fine, but thank you for caring—'

'You could take the rest of the day off to be certain,' he interrupted, as if he hadn't heard her. 'We really don't need something contagious going through the rest of the staff. We're short-handed enough as it is.'

'No. Of course not,' she agreed soberly as her fragile bubble of happiness burst, hurt that his thoughts were all for the A and E department, then cross with herself because that was the way it *should* be when he was in such a senior position. 'And I'm perfectly all right. I promise I'm not coming down with anything contagious.'

'Well, if you're sure,' he said with a frown. 'If you change your mind...'

'I won't. I'm fine,' she insisted. 'I'll see you later,' she added, suddenly desperate to get away from the stilted conversation.

She hurried back towards the board that ruled all their lives, wondering just how hard she was going to have to work to take her mind off her personal problems. For just a moment his caring attitude had made her believe that there was going to be an easy solution, that everything was going to slot into place to give her everything she'd ever dreamed of.

Now the fact that she was going to have to sit down tonight and have a proper conversation with Jake was going to loom like a black cloud in the back of her mind while she tried to find the words to break the news that she was going to have his baby.

Jake put the key in the lock and paused a moment to gather his thoughts.

He didn't know whether to groan with relief that he was finally home or whimper at the thought of yet another evening spent in Maggie's company. All he knew was that he wasn't sleeping properly and was so tired his brain wasn't functioning as well as it should.

'Just like the bad old days,' he muttered, realising that it felt just like the times during his training when he'd been rostered on call for five consecutive days and hadn't managed more than an hour's sleep at a time over the whole period.

How he'd managed to avoid killing someone when he'd been all but brain dead, he had no idea.

He drew in a deep breath to brace himself for his first sight of Maggie, not knowing whether he should pray that the place she'd been going to look at this evening was suitable. If she moved soon, it would remove the immediate temptation, but selfishly a large part of him couldn't help hoping that it took a long time so that he could hold onto every second of her company while it lasted.

As he opened the door, he played his usual guessing game.

Would Maggie be sprawled in what had become *her* corner of the settee, studying one of the weighty tomes she insisted she needed to read to keep herself up to date, or would she be busy concocting something delicious in the kitchen?

Neither, he realised with a pang of disappointment when he entered the silent room. In fact, it didn't sound as if she'd come home yet, in spite of the fact she'd left the hospital a couple of hours ago. Was she still out looking at the flat she was hoping to share?

Then a slight noise alerted him to the fact that he wasn't alone and he moved forward until he could see the whole of the settee.

His heart melted when he saw how innocent she looked, sleeping so soundly that she hadn't heard his arrival.

Before she'd left the hospital she'd changed into her usual figure-hugging jeans and a long-sleeved T-shirt, and now her usually restrained toffee-coloured hair was spread around her head like a curly halo.

She looked tired, or perhaps it was worry that pleated her forehead even in her sleep. Whatever it was, it made him want to gather her up in his arms and protect her.

He gave a silent snort of self-derision. As if feisty Maggie ffrench needed anyone to protect her. Even the discovery that her husband-to-be was a cheat and a liar hadn't kept her down for long.

That didn't stop him from wanting to be there for her.

The fact that he could never marry her didn't mean that he didn't wish it could be possible, neither did it stop him wanting her in every way a man could want the woman he loved.

Well, if the only thing he could do for her was take care of her on a day-to-day basis, so be it, and today that meant pulling his weight in the kitchen. After the day they'd had in A and E, they both needed sustenance. It certainly wasn't a job for fragile wimps.

And who knew how soon she would be moving out? If she'd liked the flat she'd looked at, this could well be the last meal they'd share together in his flat.

'Maggie?' the voice called, sounding just as sexy but far more real than it usually did in her dreams.

'Time to eat, Sleeping Beauty.'

Well, that wasn't particularly sexy. It certainly wasn't the prelude to the sort of erotic interlude she'd been enjoying in her dreams for the last few weeks.

'Hey, Rip van Winkle! Do I need to get a cold flannel? I've been slaving over a hot stove and everything's going to get cold.'

She opened her eyes and looked up into the face that had been filling her dreams.

'Jake,' she murmured sleepily, still more asleep than awake or she wouldn't even have considered reaching up to slide her fingers through the tousled thickness of his dark hair and guiding his mouth to hers.

She felt him stiffen in surprise for a fraction of a second before he responded to her kiss with an almost shocking intensity.

But the damage had been done.

In spite of the fact that she yearned for the kiss to

continue to its logical conclusion, that brief hesitation was enough to bring her to her senses.

'No,' she moaned, tightening her grip on his hair while she forced herself to turn her head away. 'We can't do this.'

'Ouch!' He winced and brought his hand up to remind her to loosen her hold, and she realised that she was almost pulling his hair out by the handful. 'I beg to differ. We can. But as to whether we should… that's a different matter.'

Filled with a wrenching sense of loss, she watched as he straightened up and took a step back from the edge of the settee.

He was right about the kisses. They could, spectacularly, and she ached to—every day of the rest of her life if only there was room in his life for her.

Maggie looked all the way up at him as he towered above her, a perfect example of masculinity, all long, lean planes and powerful muscles that she longed to explore again. But she couldn't, not with her newly discovered secret to impart. Although how she thought she could tell him such earth-shattering news while sprawled across his couch…

'Uh, did you say food was ready?' She scrambled inelegantly off the couch, wincing at the thought that she probably looked like a badly made bed. She'd intended having a shower and tidying herself up a bit before he came home, to give her confidence a bit of a boost. She'd only sat down for a moment while she'd tried to plan what to say, but tiredness had descended over her like a heavy blanket and she hadn't been able to keep her eyes open.

So here she was, with a fuzzy brain and an empty stomach. She couldn't possibly tell him now, she reasoned silently as she sat at the inviting table and reached for a piece of hot crusty garlic bread. After they'd eaten would be far better, when he'd had some time to unwind from work.

And, if she was honest with herself, she would have to admit that she was putting off the moment of truth. She'd heard far too many accounts of unplanned pregnancies destroying relationships and she had no idea how Jake was going to react, especially as he'd been at great pains to tell her, right from the first, that there was no prospect of marriage.

Added to that was the detail that they didn't really have a relationship beyond the fact that they were colleagues and friends...apart from that one night. Even in her thoughts she refused to call it a one-night-stand. That was far too tacky a term for the magic they'd shared.

'So, what did you think about it?' Jake prompted, and left her wondering if she'd been so busy wool-gathering she'd completely missed a whole conversation.

'What did I think about what?' She felt the heat washing over her cheeks and hoped she hadn't made a monumental fool of herself. What topic had he shifted to while her mind had been reliving *that* night?

'About the flat you went to see this evening,' he said patiently. 'You were going to see it when you left work, remember?'

'Oh, lord, I completely forgot!' she wailed, and leapt up from the table. 'Where's my bag? I put the telephone number in it. If I give them a ring, perhaps I could go over there now.'

Impatiently, she tipped the contents of her handbag

out onto the table beside her plate and found the elusive scrap of paper.

Two minutes later she was shovelling everything back into the bag with a despondent droop to her shoulders.

'I'm so sorry, Jake,' she murmured guiltily. 'When I didn't turn up, someone else snapped it up straight away. I could actually hear them moving in as I was talking on the phone.' She dumped the bag on the floor beside her chair and slumped into it, planting her elbows on the table as she clutched at her head.

'Hey, what are you apologising for? There'll be other places,' he encouraged.

'But *when*?' she demanded. 'That was the first affordable place I've come across in weeks! *And* it was within walking distance of the hospital, so I could have saved money on transport, too.'

'So, you're telling me you're desperate to get out of here, are you?' he teased. 'I didn't think I was that bad.'

'That's not the point,' she argued, frustrated that her whole life was in such turmoil and close to tears. 'One way or another, every one of my plans is falling apart. Just a few weeks ago it looked as if I was going to have everything—the job I wanted, working with a great group of colleagues, a husband-to-be who already had two lovely children and wanted more, and a lovely home to move into. And now everything's gone.'

'Everything?' Jake questioned softly, the intensity of his gaze bringing her up sharply. 'If you could magically go back in time, would you really rather have gone ahead with the wedding? Would you rather not have overheard that conversation and be living your perfect life?'

Maggie sighed heavily. 'Damn you for spoiling a good rant, Jake Lascelles. Of course I wouldn't rather have married the rat, just to have the appearance of my dream. I still want the real thing.'

And more than ever, since she'd been sharing his flat, she knew that he was the person she really loved, the reason why she'd been happy enough to marry a man she didn't really love when she couldn't have the man she really wanted.

Jake had warned her from the start that he wasn't the marrying kind, but did he still feel the same way? Surely this time they'd spent together had showed him that they would be good together, and that night had certainly demonstrated that they were sexually compatible.

And in the middle of all that she realised that she'd actually forgotten that there would be a permanent reminder of that night, that she had something earth-shattering to tell him.

Suddenly all the apprehension and excitement that had been building up in equal quantities since she'd seen that tell-tale stripe on the test kit spilled over.

Without giving herself time to recall the careful speech she'd composed, she opened her mouth and let the first words that came into her head spill out.

'Jake, what would you say about having a baby?' she blurted.

'A baby?' He blinked, obviously startled by the abrupt question.

'*Your* baby,' she prompted expectantly, knowing she was doing this all wrong but unable to back out now. Her heart was nearly beating its way out of her chest as she waited for his response. Of course it would be a shock, but she knew what a good man he was. It wouldn't take long before he was as delighted as she was, and maybe…just maybe…

'My baby?' he echoed softly, and his eyes darkened for a fraction of a second before he brought the shutters down. 'Look, Maggie, I know you were badly let down by Liam, and that the two of us…went a bit further than we should have that night, but I told you up front that I won't be getting married.'

'But I wasn't asking you to marry me,' she retorted stiffly, completely sidetracked. She was stung by his easy dismissal of what they'd shared when it had meant so much to her, not least because it had resulted in the precious embryo already developing deep inside her. She suddenly realised that he still hadn't commented on that announcement, and wondered if she hadn't made herself clear. 'Jake, I'm not making any demands. I just wanted to tell you that we—'

'Maggie, I know that we work well together,' he interrupted, clearly agitated by the direction the conversation was taking. 'Over the last two years we've built up a good relationship, and you're a very desirable woman, but you want to surround yourself with a family and I *can't*—' he pulled himself up sharply, almost as if stopping himself from revealing too much, then finished, 'I'm sorry, but I'm just not cut out to be a family man.'

It took Maggie several seconds before she could speak, her throat completely closed by the threat of tears, but finally she broke the tension-filled silence.

'I suppose that's what they call putting all your cards on the table, so I'll try to do the same,' she said, hoping the tremble in her voice wasn't as obvious as it felt to her.

The fact that he'd said she was a very desirable woman was a real boost to her ego. It was far more personal than anything he'd ever said before or after that one night. Unfortunately it was totally overshadowed by the fact that he believed there was no room for her in his career-orientated life.

'I might have been a bit clumsy about it,' she began shakily, 'and I certainly wouldn't want you to feel that I was presuming on your good nature as...' She paused, looking for the right term. It wouldn't do either of them any favours if she called him a one-night stand, or referred to the fact that he was her boss. She certainly couldn't say that he hadn't warned her right from the first that marriage and family weren't on his agenda, so she couldn't cry foul now.

'As my temporary landlord,' she compromised. 'I'm certainly not telling you this to angle for a more permanent arrangement. I promise that I *am* looking to move out into alternative accommodation as soon as possible, but I thought it was only right to let you know that I took a test at the hospital today and...and I found out that...I'm pregnant.'

CHAPTER SIX

JAKE was shocked into speechlessness. It was the very last thing he'd expected, and spelt the end of even the most tentative of his dreams.

His brain was empty of everything apart from the fact that there was a baby growing inside Maggie…a baby that could never be a part of his life and would ultimately take Maggie away from him.

It was pure selfishness on his part that his first re-action was denial. He'd loved Maggie for so long that he didn't want anything to come between them, es-pecially now, when she was sharing his home. It was the closest he would ever come to marriage and, apart from the frustration of not sharing her bed, he was savouring every moment.

Of course he'd known from the first that sharing his flat would only be a temporary measure, just until she got her life back on track again. It would only be a matter of time before her salary rose closer to his and she would be able to afford to buy something of her own.

What was going to happen now?

'Maggie?' He finally turned to speak to her, need-ing some answers to the questions boring holes in his head and his heart, but she wasn't there any more. For just a moment he was paralysed by the fear that she'd left the flat altogether, let down by the fact that he hadn't offered any support, then he heard the sound of the shower and almost collapsed with relief.

'She's still here,' he breathed, and lowered himself to the arm of the settee on shaky legs, grateful that he hadn't blown it completely. He still had tonight to get his thoughts together. 'I can talk to her in the morning.'

Two days later he was still trying to pin her down, and the longer it went on the more he wondered exactly what he'd said to her that she should be avoiding him so deliberately.

He'd barely come to terms with her announcement even now, and certainly couldn't remember what he'd said to her—if anything.

He couldn't remember much more about what she'd said either. Had she told him whether she was going to continue with her job as soon as her maternity leave was over? Or was she going to wait until the child was older before she returned to her profession?

Most importantly, had she told him whether she was going to be getting married after all? And, if so, to whom?

He knew the baby couldn't be Liam's, but he hadn't realised that she'd started another relationship since their night together.

He snorted in derision. How could he know when he'd spent the last few weeks trying so hard not to let Maggie know how he felt about her that he'd actually taken to avoiding her—and in a busy A and E department that was no mean feat.

Now she was employing the same avoidance tactics, including changing her shifts so that she arrived home long after he'd gone to bed.

Not that he was sleeping very well, as evidenced

by the dark shadows under his eyes and the brain full of cotton wool, and while he could put up with looking haggard, his professionalism wouldn't allow him to compromise patient safety.

'Enough is enough!' he muttered into the echoing silence of the staff washroom, staring into the mirror at his hangdog face and wondering where his backbone had been for the last couple of days.

It had been bad enough when he'd only had to catch sight of Maggie in the department to find himself imagining her without a stitch of clothing, her neatly confined hair tousled at the end of a particularly energetic tumble in the sheets and her eyes darkly drowsy with satisfaction. Then, avoiding her had been the only way to preserve his sanity, but the last few days had been something else entirely.

'Face it, Lascelles, hiding your head in the sand isn't solving anything, and it won't make her pregnancy disappear.'

It also wouldn't stop his heart from aching at the thought that Maggie was going to finally be beyond his reach. Not that he'd ever entertained more than self-indulgent fantasies about the two of them being together once she'd told him about her dream of having the perfect family, but once she was married he wouldn't even feel comfortable about fantasising about her any more.

'Do I need any more evidence that my brains have been scrambled by the wretched woman?' he groaned when he tried to unravel that complicated thought, reaching for his shrilling pager at the same time. 'I need to sort this out today.'

In fact, tonight would make more sense, when there

wasn't the possibility of half of their colleagues eavesdropping on the conversation.

Tonight he was going to make certain that he arrived home at a reasonable hour and he was going to do what he should have done when Maggie had first made her announcement—he was going to sit her down and ask her the questions that had been burning a hole in his gut ever since.

Two days after she'd made her announcement, Maggie still didn't know whether to laugh, cry, or indulge in an utterly childish tantrum, complete with drumming heels and high-pitched shrieks.

The stunned expression on Jake's face would certainly have been comical enough, if it hadn't been so sad. It certainly hadn't been the overjoyed look of a man happy to be told he was going to be a father.

'Well, I certainly didn't achieve it without his input,' she muttered, then had to stifle a giggle when she realised her unintentional double entendre.

Then she remembered their conversation two years ago, and the way he had been at such pains to tell her that marriage wasn't on the cards for him, and she couldn't help feeling guilty that she had thrown such a disruptive spanner in his works.

It had been just as much her responsibility as his to take care of protection on the night they'd spent together, and at least she'd had a few hours to get used to the idea that she was pregnant. It was hardly fair to judge him by his initial reaction to such a bombshell.

'Bombshells and spanners? How many more similes can I use to describe one situation?' she muttered as she rummaged through the kitchen cupboard. Somewhere in here she was sure she'd seen…

'Ah, here they are!' She brandished the packet of ginger biscuits she'd unearthed from the back corner, then grabbed the bottle of fizzy glucose drink. 'Tomorrow morning I'll find out if Mrs Stoddard was right.' It was amazing the topics that could be covered in the course of an emergency room consultation. The heavily pregnant mother of one little patient had regaled her at length with her tried-and-tested remedy for morning sickness while avoiding watching her son have a ragged head laceration stitched—hence the ginger biscuits and fizz.

The fact that she'd waited in vain for Jake to arrive so that she could talk to him was something she refused to think about. For now, it was enough that she was going to bed knowing that when she woke up it would be to the prospect of nausea and a quick run to the bathroom.

She emerged from the kitchen clutching the drink and biscuits like trophies and cannoned straight into Jake.

'Oof!'

'Watch out!'

In spite of both their efforts, the plastic container of fizz landed on the biscuits, smashing one and splitting the other.

'Drat! What a mess!' Maggie wailed, bending to retrieve the plastic bottle before it could completely empty its sticky contents all over the floor.

Jake stooped to the same task and they hit heads with a solid thump.

'Ouch!' Maggie sat down with a thud, her head ringing with the impact.

'I'm sorry, Maggie!' Jake only just managed to stay upright and quickly reached out to help her to her feet. 'Are you all right?'

'Nothing broken. Which is more than I can say for my biscuits.' She scowled, thinking of the trip she was going to have to make to the little shop nearby to replace both drink and biscuits. At least it stayed open later than most, even if it wasn't a particularly salubrious area for late-night shopping. She grabbed a cloth from the kitchen and began to mop up the debris.

'What was all this in aid of?' he questioned as he bent down to help, scooping up the soggy biscuits and dumping them in the bin. 'Was it a midnight feast for one or do I get an invitation to join you?'

Jake's cheerful teasing unexpectedly caught her on the raw. She straightened up sharply, the dripping cloth disgustingly sticky in her hand.

'If you'd been home a little earlier, there'd have been more than a packet of biscuits on offer, and before you do the usual male hormonal thing, I *don't* mean sex!'

His startled look was mixed with guilt and an unexpected dash of hurt that suddenly made her feel like the worst of shrews. *She* was the interloper here, not Jake. If he wanted to stay out all night, that was his prerogative. The fact was that she'd wanted to talk to him…to clear the air between them and find out how he felt about the baby now that he'd had some time to think about it.

'Look, I'm sorry,' she apologised hastily. 'I shouldn't have said that. I'm just tired and out of sorts and I really needed those for tomorrow morning.'

'It is late when you have days as busy as ours,' he

agreed. 'I had intended coming home earlier, but we had an influx of young bucks taking their mate out on a stag night and ended up in a bottle fight. We could have done with your steady hand to put the groom's face back together again.'

'Oh, lord,' she breathed. 'Was he badly hurt?' She could just imagine how much irrigation it had taken to make certain that there was no glass left in the wounds before suturing could even begin.

'He was lucky. There was no apparent neurological damage, but he certainly won't want to look at his wedding photos very often,' Jake said wryly.

'If his bride-to-be doesn't change her mind when she sees him,' Maggie pointed out.

'Just because he's scarred? Would something like that put *you* off?'

He knew that it was Liam's lies rather than his vasectomy that had stopped her marrying his friend, but there was a strange intensity in his gaze that made her wonder if there was something personal in the question—except she knew Jake didn't have a disfiguring scar anywhere on that gorgeous body. She'd seen every inch of it that memorable night and in all her dreams since.

'I would have thought you'd know me better than that by now,' she reminded him. 'The thing that would worry me far more than any physical disfigurement was whether the man was prone to fighting and whether he had any scruples about using his fists on women and children. Now,' she continued briskly, turning towards her bedroom, 'as a result of dropping that lot all over the floor, I'm going to have to do a quick trip to the corner shop.'

'You're going this late at night? Surely there's

something else in the cupboard that would do until we do some shopping to replace it tomorrow?'

'Actually, no.' She felt the slow wash of heat across her face that told her she wasn't quite as blasé as she thought she was about bodily functions, especially when they were her own. And as for mentioning a symptom of the very topic she'd hoped to raise with him… 'They were ginger biscuits, and you haven't got any more of them in the cupboard.'

'So?' His frown told her he hadn't picked up on the significance.

'Ginger is supposed to help combat nausea, and so is that brand of fizzy glucose drink. I was going to put them beside my bed ready for the morning. One of my patients suggested it. She said it was the only combination that worked for her and I thought I'd give it a go to see if…' Too much information, she realized, and bit her tongue to stop herself chattering, then finished lamely, 'I'll just go and get my purse and—'

'I'll go,' he said shortly, and was already halfway to the door before she could draw a breath. 'I won't be long.'

'You don't have to…' She was speaking to empty air, and when she remembered the expression on his face when she'd mentioned nausea she had to stifle a giggle. For all that he was a highly qualified doctor, he'd actually looked petrified at the idea that she might be sick…or had that been fear of the pregnancy that was causing the nausea?

Well, whatever it was, she knew that he wasn't going to be gone long, and even though she'd given up on the idea of waiting up for him in favour of having an early night, it would be worth staying up now just to pin Jake down.

That idea made her laugh out loud. As if she'd have a chance of pinning down someone that big and fit and muscular if he didn't want to be held.

Still, they needed to clear the air, even if it was just to come to an agreement to table a discussion for later, when he'd had enough time to sort out his thoughts and feelings.

Suddenly, completely out of the blue, she felt the need to speak to her family. It was ridiculous really, considering the rest of them all lived on the other side of the world now. And it wasn't as if they'd had much time for her when they *had* lived in England. Big brother David had always been the apple of his mother's eye, right from the moment he was born and the focus of all his father's thwarted ambitions.

When David had moved to New Zealand with his new wife, Maggie could have made a fortune on betting how long it would be before her parents sold up and followed them south of the equator. The fact that shortly after they'd arrived they'd announced that their first grandchild was on the way had only made it happen faster.

She was still standing in the middle of the room locked in her memories when the sound of Jake's key in the lock sent her pulse into overdrive.

'There you go.' He held a small bag stuffed full of his recent purchases out towards her, then paused, instantly concerned. 'What's the matter? Are you ill?'

'No. I'm fine,' she said airily, feeling distinctly foolish. She was twenty-nine years old, for heaven's sake. She shouldn't be reacting like a little child wanting its mother.

'Maggie?' He fixed her with those dark blue eyes, and the concern in them broke down a barrier she'd never breached before, even though they'd shared more than a few heart-to-hearts over the last two years.

'I was just being stupid…childish.' She tried to sound dismissive but the weight of years of feeling as if she just didn't matter was too overwhelming to bear any longer. 'Why did it always seem as if David had it all?' she blurted out, startled to feel the heat of impending tears. 'Was it just the green eyes of a younger sibling?'

Suddenly Jake was there, wrapping her in the comfort of strong male arms and asking just enough questions to prompt her into pouring out the whole sorry story.

She told him of a childhood spent following in the footsteps of her popular elder brother, having to sit quietly at parent-teacher meetings where her own achievements were completely ignored in favour of a paean of praise for David. The fact that he'd done nothing to encourage it and had even done his best to deflect some of his parents' attention onto her hadn't made the situation any better.

Finally she'd stopped trying to compete, but by that time she had already embarked on her medical training—following in David's footsteps again—and had discovered that she loved it and, what was more, was good at it.

In fact, now that she thought about it, the close-knit community of the hospital was probably the closest she'd come to having a caring family around her.

'So I've always had to get on with things by myself,' she said, trying for a bracing tone. 'It was stupid to think that phoning my family would make anything better.'

Certainly they wouldn't have listened the way Jake had, totally non-judgmentally. Perhaps that was a good indicator for their own upcoming conversation.

Just the thought of it was enough to start the tension building again, and she had to force herself to step out of the circle of Jake's comforting arms before he recognised the fact.

Immediately she missed his warmth, and the feeling of unconditional support, but this was something she was going to have to do on her own. Maybe if she could keep her nerves under control, she could stop it turning into a confrontation…but knowing that her pregnancy was not what Jake had wanted in his life wasn't going to make anything easy.

'Anyway, that's more than enough about me. What on earth did you buy?' she demanded, looking round for the abandoned bag of shopping. 'You were only supposed to be getting two items.'

'Well…' he said, looking distinctly sheepish. 'The woman in the shop suggested that if the ginger biscuits and fizz didn't work you could try old-fashioned ginger beer, or there's a range of fruit teas that do a ginger one especially for nausea.'

Her eyes were riveted on the sweep of colour highlighting his cheekbones, and she was touched that he could be so thoughtful in spite of his less-than-welcoming initial reaction to her announcement.

'Thank you.' She smiled wryly. 'But I really hope the morning sickness isn't going to be bad enough to warrant this many remedies.'

'And you don't have to worry about looking for a flat,' he announced. 'Being pregnant is enough stress on its own. You don't need to add house-hunting to it when you're already settled in here— unless you've already decided to move in with…someone else?' he added with a significant glance in the direction of her mercifully flat abdomen.

Maggie didn't know when she'd ever received so many mixed signals in a single conversation, and still wasn't sure whether she should be laughing manically or releasing high-pressure steam from a vent in the top of her head.

One minute he was melting her heart with his thoughtfulness, the next he was autocratically telling her that she should stop house-hunting, and then he seemed to be hinting…what? That there was some doubt about the paternity of her baby? That she might be moving in with some other man?

'Would you prefer that?' she demanded sharply, hanging onto her temper by a thread. She was in love with the man, for heaven's sake, and had been for two years. And in spite of the fact that she'd been willing to marry Liam, to have the family she'd always craved, it was Jake's baby that she'd wanted and it was his baby that was now slowly but surely developing deep inside her.

'What?'

'Would you prefer it if I moved in with someone else? Because if you're only offering me a place out of charity—'

'No! That wasn't what I meant at all.' He rammed his fingers through his hair, leaving it standing up in endearing spikes. 'It's just that I didn't want you to feel that you *had* to stay here just because you started off that way as a stop-gap measure.'

'And?'

'And what?' he echoed with a frown.

'You didn't answer my question,' she pointed out. 'Would you prefer it if I moved in with someone else?'

'No, I wouldn't,' he said with reassuring firmness, his eyes seeming to meet hers with complete honesty.

'Are you sure? After all, you moved here to get away from all the communal living where we were before.'

'I'm sure,' he said patiently, then grinned. 'In fact, I'm quite enjoying it—and not just for the fact that you're doing so many of the everyday chores.'

'You do your share,' she pointed out fairly. 'And it's a real treat to have a meal cooked for me sometimes.'

'So there's no problem with staying?'

Maggie should have expected that. Jake always did like all the ends tied up neatly, whether at work or in his private life. This time she had more than a loose end of her own left flapping in the breeze.

'As long as you don't have a problem with the pregnancy,' she said baldly.

'Why should I have a problem with it?' Instantly her frustration level rose. The infuriating man had actually managed to look convincingly puzzled.

'You mean, apart from the fact that you've always been at great pains to tell me that you are never going to get married? And there's also the fact that you're never going to have children because you don't believe in having children outside marriage.'

'I didn't exactly put it like that,' he argued, clearly uncomfortable with the direction the conversation was taking.

'Near as dammit,' she shot back, hurt all over again

that he'd been able to dismiss her so easily when she'd been half in love with him right from the beginning. 'Jake, you've been keeping me at arm's length for two years, and now we're living together—or sharing a flat, at least—and I'm pregnant.'

Even as she spoke she saw something change in his expression, that same something that she'd seen at regular intervals over the last two years, when he'd been confronted by a particularly puzzling set of symptoms and had suddenly managed to unravel their significance to come to a diagnosis.

'So, let's go for broke, then, Maggie,' he said cheerfully. 'Let's get married.'

'What?' she gaped at him, then laughed. 'Don't be ridiculous! You don't want to get married—remember? You've been telling everyone that ever since I've known you.'

'I can change my mind, can't I?' he challenged. 'It's not just a female prerogative in these days of equal opportunities.'

She refused to be sidetracked by another rehashing of the battle of the sexes. 'I might believe you'd changed your mind if you'd actually sounded as if you meant it,' she pointed out, even as a frantic voice in the back of her head was screaming at her to accept.

'And anyway,' she continued, deliberately stifling the temptation before she had a chance to act on it, even though her heart was breaking with disappointment, 'I *haven't* changed my mind. When I marry, my husband and I will be in love with each other—it won't be some sort of misguided charity case just so the baby won't be illegitimate. That would be doomed to failure as soon as you came to your senses.'

'Me and my big mouth!'

Jake stared up at the ceiling and groaned. It was gone midnight and he was no closer to sleep than when he'd come to bed.

'I can't believe I said it!' he exclaimed, and when he thought of the *way* he'd said it, he should hardly be surprised that she'd laughed in disbelief.

The thought had just popped into his head, and for one blinding moment it had seemed so *right*, so much the perfect solution to everything, and...well, almost before he'd realised he was going to speak, he'd blurted out a proposal.

'If you could call that a proposal,' he muttered darkly, feeling the unfamiliar heat of a blush surge up his throat and into his cheeks when he remembered his total lack of finesse.

'The last of the great romantics, that's me,' he said in disgust. 'The fact that I've never had any practice is no excuse. No wonder she turned me down.'

But the more he thought about it, the more he realised that there had been something far more than the lack of romance in his proposal that had made her refuse. Was it Liam? Had she realised that she was more in love with the man than she'd thought? Was she regretting giving him his marching orders, especially now that she was pregnant?

'And that's another thing,' he mused aloud. 'She's never said who's fathered the baby.' And, even with a case of jealousy bad enough to turn his face toxic green for the next millennium, he couldn't think of anyone in the hospital that she'd been especially close to—apart from that one night with him.

'She's been living here, for heaven's sake!' he told the shadows. 'I'd have known if she'd invited anyone back here, and we work together all day. It couldn't be anyone in A and E or the hospital grapevine would have got hold of it.'

Anyway, he couldn't imagine Maggie sloping off into the sluices for a clandestine liaison during her shift. It just wasn't her style. Not that he hadn't imagined it a time or two with himself playing a leading role, but that had been sheer frustration painting pictures. He'd never have taken such a chance, even if she'd been willing. He had the feeling that with the particularly narrow-minded people at the top of the hospital hierarchy it would have been professional suicide if they'd been caught.

A sudden thought hit him with devastating impact.

'The hospital grapevine!' he groaned, his brain leaping forward a few weeks to the time when Maggie's condition would become obvious. 'Everyone will be playing the guessing game and counting back on their fingers. Her reputation will be trashed.'

The thoughts went round and round in his head for at least another hour, and with every passing moment he became more sure that his spur-of-the-moment solution really was the only answer to the situation. Never mind the fact that it was what he'd longed for, even when he'd known that it could never happen.

'She needs a husband and the baby needs a father,' he enumerated softly, marshalling his arguments aloud for the first time, wryly aware that this was what he should have done before he'd opened his mouth in the first place. 'We've become good friends

over the last two years, and there's no doubt that
we're sexually compatible…'

Predictably, his blood pressure rose the moment
those images surfaced in his mind and he had to quell
them ruthlessly.

'Well, perhaps that's something I don't need to
spell out,' he muttered grimly as he fought to keep
his thoughts on track. Neither would he be pouring
out the fact that he'd been attracted to her right from
her first day in A and E, and that the attraction had
quickly deepened into a love that he'd never believed
could end up in happily-ever-after. That would have
to be his secret, too, until she'd had a chance to see
if the friendship she felt for him could grow into an
answering love.

'So, where do I go from here?' he mused, calmer
now that he'd come to a tentative decision. 'How do
I persuade someone as stubborn as Maggie that marrying me would be the best way out of her dilemma?
How do I persuade her that I'd be a good bet as a
husband and father when I've spent the last two years
telling her that it's the last thing I want in my life?
How do I know I'd be any good at it, anyway?'

Then he thought about the trusting way she'd allowed him to hold her while she'd spilled out her hurt
at her parents' unthinking cruelty, and remembered
the surge of emotion that would have prompted him
to slay dragons for her if it would have taken her
unhappiness away, and he didn't think he'd have any
problem being a caring husband. And when his imagination conjured up a picture of a child that was a
miniature of Maggie, perfect right down to her toffee-
coloured hair and changeable blue-green eyes, he

didn't have any more doubts about his willingness to learn how to be a father either.

'And it wouldn't matter who the biological father was. He or she would be *my* child as soon as I put my ring on Maggie's finger,' he said aloud, unsurprised when it sounded like a promise.

But that still left him with the problem of how to make it happen.

'How does *any* man get a woman to accept his proposal?' he mused, and then the obvious struck him right between the eyes. 'I'm going to have to go right back to the beginning, aren't I? I'm going to have to… What? Date her? No. That's not it exactly, because we've already gone beyond a first date and holding hands—gone beyond French kissing, too…' He chuckled when he realised that any kiss from Maggie would be a ffrench kiss, then grew serious again with the stern reminder that his future happiness was at stake here.

'No, it might sound old-fashioned, and I haven't got a clue how to go about it, but I'm going to have to court Maggie—until ''yes'' is the only possible answer.'

CHAPTER SEVEN

'COFFEE, Maggie?' Jake offered solicitously as she slumped tiredly into the nearest available chair.

She glared at him, longing to snap his head off but unable to say a word with so many colleagues around.

She was beginning to wish she hadn't told him about the baby until her increasing size made the fact impossible to hide. Who could have guessed that the news of her pregnancy would cause him to have a complete change of character?

Or had it been the spineless way she'd blubbered in his arms and spilled the pathetic details of her dysfunctional family?

Whatever the reason, ever since that night he'd been treating her differently, and it was getting... what? Annoying? Embarrassing?

It seemed that every time she turned round, there he was, offering assistance, advice, a cup of coffee—even though he knew that the very smell of it made her want to rush off to hang her head over the nearest toilet.

Perhaps it was a mixture of frustration and disappointment. Frustration that he could never be what she'd always wanted him to be—the man who would love her and cherish her for a lifetime—and disappointment that she'd even lost the Jake she'd had before—the friend she'd always been able to confide in.

She didn't know this Jake at all and for that she felt guilty, certain that it had been her revelation of his impending fatherhood that had changed him. Not that he'd ever mentioned the fact, unless she took his out-of-the-blue marriage proposal as an acknowledge ment of responsibility.

'Maggie? Coffee?' he prompted, and she shook her head silently, far too involved with her thoughts to think about the consequences of trying to drink the beverage she still craved.

She still couldn't believe that he'd actually proposed! Jake! Dr My-profession-is-all-I-need-in-my-life Lascelles.

Why had he done it, for heaven's sake?

It certainly wasn't because he'd suddenly discovered that he was madly in love with her, that was for certain. In lust, maybe, but even that was doubtful considering he'd barely looked at her since she'd moved in with him, let alone chased her all over the flat slavering with desire.

'Here,' said a voice right beside her, and she nearly leapt out of her skin.

'What? Oh, it's you,' she groaned when she realised it was Jake standing there, offering her a glass of orange juice.

'I thought this might be more acceptable,' he explained quietly. 'And it will boost your vitamins.'

Suddenly, she was close to tears. This was the Jake she'd fallen in love with, the caring, considerate man who would go out of his way to help anyone. This was the man who, against all common sense, she wanted to marry, regardless of his reasons for offering.

'Jake…' What on earth could she say to him when any number of ears could be listening?

The phone rang stridently and they all groaned as one of the people closest to it lifted the receiver.

Conversations were put on hold while they listened with bated breath, then there was a concerted groan at the news of yet another pile-up on the nearby motorway—one of the penalties of a hospital situated so close to such a major route.

'Thank goodness we cleared the backlog from the collapsed scaffolding on the building site,' Jake commented. 'How many vehicles involved?' He straightened to his full height and strode towards the nurse relaying the messages, and Maggie couldn't help noticing that he seemed unusually weary. In spite of their differences her heart went out to him and she wished there was something she could do to ease the pressures on him.

Would marriage help him? She longed to take care of him, and she had enough love in her heart for both of them, but she would be fooling herself if she thought that a long-term relationship between them could work when he couldn't even bring himself to mention their child.

'Only one, but there are more than a dozen casualties. It was a minibus full of rugby fans. ETA for the first batch is ten to fifteen minutes.'

She quickly downed the drink Jake had brought her. There was no telling when she might have time for another one and she had more than her own health to think about now.

Everyone was grumbling as they left the room, but there was purpose in their direction as each went to do their part to check that the department was ready for the influx.

Maggie arrived just in time to hear Lina Mackey

giving her usual speech to the patients waiting in Reception.

'We have patients coming in from an accident on the motorway,' she announced. 'This means that any patients already waiting will have to wait even longer if their problem is less serious.'

'But we were here first,' shouted one patient belligerently. 'These new buggers should get to the back of the queue.'

'Some of them might,' Lina agreed pleasantly. 'But an accident and emergency department can't be run on a first-come, first-served basis. We have to treat people based on the severity of their conditions. If you have been assessed by the triage nurse your name will be on the board and I'm afraid you're just going to have to be patient.'

Having been firmly but politely put in his place, the man subsided, but Maggie could see that he definitely wasn't happy. She wouldn't be in the least bit surprised if he caused trouble later on.

In the meantime, she could hear the sound of approaching sirens and turned to join the rest of the teams making their way towards the emergency entrance.

The back doors of the ambulance swung wide and the first thing she heard was the sound of singing.

'What on earth…?' exclaimed one of the waiting staff.

'Rugby supporters,' another said dismissively, as if it was only to be expected. 'Either their team won, in which case they've been celebrating, or they lost, in which case they've been drowning their sorrows.'

Even as he was speaking the first patient was being

unloaded, a burly-looking man with a wonderful tenor voice richly tinged with a Welsh accent.

Unfortunately, his long scarf proudly striped with his team colours was marred by great patches of bright blood.

'No apparent injuries apart from a large scalp wound,' Maggie heard the bemused paramedic report. 'He's drunk as a skunk and totally oblivious to any pain—refused any analgesia.'

The man was still singing loudly as he was wheeled out of sight and Maggie stepped forward to receive her charge.

'This one's similarly well anaesthetised—so much so that he was perfectly happy to try to walk home on a broken ankle.'

'Ouch!' Maggie winced. 'How far did he get?' And just how much further damage had he done to himself in his attempt?

'A matter of yards rather than miles, mostly because he couldn't stand up straight even with two good feet.' The paramedic chuckled. 'You know, it's the most amazing thing I've ever seen. There was the minibus in a field, having rolled several times down an embankment, and this is the most serious injury we've come across so far.'

'What? That's impossible!' Maggie exclaimed as she paced the trolley into the department and directed it into the nearest trauma room.

'Not if you're that well oiled, apparently,' Jake said with a chuckle, overhearing her comment and looking up from his own charge. 'It looks as if they've bounced around inside the vehicle rather than broken, as relaxed as rag dolls.'

'It's all Taff's fault,' piped up Maggie's patient,

demonstrating that there was little wrong with his faculties as he followed the conversation going on around him. 'He wanted to go for a—' He stopped suddenly, as though only just noticing that there were ladies present. 'He'd been drinking a bit, see, and needed to get rid of a bit of it in a bit of a hurry, see. And when the driver said he couldn't pull across onto the hard shoulder just for him to find a convenient tree, Taff grabbed the wheel and the next thing we knew we were going round like cement in a mixer.'

He reached down to grab Maggie's arm as she looked a bit closer at his leg.

'How is Taff, my lovely? Have you seen him?' he asked anxiously, his voice sounding slurred for the first time.

'I haven't, Gwilym, but I've been in here with you,' she explained gently. 'There are several other rooms with other teams of doctors and nurses taking care of your friends.'

'It would be a dreadful thing if he were hurt,' Gwilym said seriously, clearly having to concentrate to form the words. 'He's our only bass baritone and there's a big competition coming up soon, see. It just wouldn't be the same without Taff and that's a fact.'

'We'll do our best for all of you,' she promised, giving his hand a reassuring pat. 'Now, the radiographer is going to take a picture of that ankle of yours, so you just lie nice and still till she's finished.'

Maggie hurried to get behind the protective screen before the first X-ray was taken, conscious for the first time of the many potential dangers to her unborn child. At this early stage of development, exposure to radiation could result in gross irreversible malformations that could threaten the baby's life.

She returned to Gwilym's side as soon as the plates had been taken, her eyes already scanning the monitors to check his vital signs. There was something nagging at her...something not quite right with his condition... He was slurring his words, but that was to be expected if he'd been imbibing that freely, but even so...

'Damn!' Even as she watched he slid into unconsciousness and one of the monitors sounded its shrill warning. 'What's his blood sugar level? I think he's going into a hyper coma.'

'I didn't see any bracelet or pendant alerting us to the fact he's diabetic!' exclaimed the nurse who'd removed his clothing. 'And he certainly didn't mention it to anyone or it would have been in the paramedic's notes when he handed him over to us.'

'There's no time for recriminations,' Maggie stated firmly. 'Let's get it sorted, fast. What's his reading?'

'It says twenty-three!' The disbelief was obvious in the shocked voice. 'I'll check it again.'

Maggie was equally concerned if the figure was correct, as a normal reading should have been under seven. 'Let's get that insulin into him now. The longer it stays that high, the more damage it's doing to him.'

And the last thing he needed was a systemic problem when he wanted his body in tip-top condition to heal broken bones, she added silently. Had the silly man been so excited by the match that he'd completely forgotten to take his tablets? She would have thought it would be harder to forget to give himself an injection, if that had become part of his daily routine, but there was no evidence in any of the usual sites that he'd been accustomed to long-term self-injecting.

'Of course, the next problem will be the timing of sending him up to Theatre,' she muttered as she took a quick look at the finished X-rays.

Jake had joined her at the view-box and winced at the extent of the damage.

'At a guess, that's going to need extensive pinning, and I don't think the anaesthetist is going to be very happy about putting him under until his blood's been sorted out.'

'On the other hand, the longer it takes before the jigsaw is put back together, the less likely it is that it's going to heal well.'

'Catch twenty-two!' they chorused, and shared a grin that lifted Maggie's spirits.

This was what had been missing from their relationship over the last few days and weeks—the light-hearted banter and exchanges that were part and parcel not only of their working environment but also their friendship.

This time, though, Maggie realised that there was something different about Jake, and it wasn't until she looked closely that she could see that the change was in his eyes. For the first time that she could remember, the deep blue had lost the shadows that had always haunted them. Now there was a gleam that almost spoke of excitement and was certainly filled with purpose.

'Hey, we're both due to finish together tonight. How about stopping off for a meal instead of going straight back home?' he suggested, much to her surprise. In all the time they'd known each other they'd never gone out together—as part of a larger group, perhaps, when celebrating a milestone of a fellow member of staff, but never just the two of them.

For a moment she was so taken aback by the idea that she nearly turned him down, but then the chance to spend some special time with him caught her imagination and she couldn't resist.

'Where were you thinking of going?' she asked, but his reply was interrupted by a voice calling for Maggie.

'He's back with us!'

Maggie had been so focused on her private conversation that she couldn't think what the nurse was talking about. She turned reluctantly to ask, and saw that her patient's eyes were open again.

'Hello, Gwilym. How are you feeling?'

Automatically she reached for his wrist, in spite of the fact that the bank of monitors were displaying everything she needed to know about his current status.

'A bit woozy, my lovely. And very thirsty.' He paused and frowned as if he was having trouble gathering his thoughts. 'In fact, I've had a powerful thirst for several days now, otherwise I wouldn't have drunk so much beer today. I'm not usually a drinking man.'

'A good job in your condition,' Maggie agreed, pleased to see that he was looking brighter by the minute. It was amazing what a dose of insulin and some water could do to a sugar-laden system. 'And how long have you been a diabetic, Gwilym?'

'Diabetic? I'm not diabetic!' he scoffed. 'I've never had a day's illness in my life. In fact, I weigh less now than I did when I got married ten years ago, and

I'm still just as fit as when I used to play rugby myself.'

He was built on strong, wiry lines, it was true, but now that Maggie looked at him his skin had the peculiar texture of someone severely dehydrated, and it didn't look good on someone still in their thirties.

'Have you lost much weight recently?' she prompted, knowing that was one of the signs of the onset of insulin-dependent diabetes.

'About two stones, and I'm eating like a horse, too,' he said proudly.

Maggie smiled wryly, knowing that her patient didn't realise that every word was helping to confirm the diagnosis of IDD.

Well, there was little more she could do for him in A and E. Treatment of his condition was going to be a long-term job, and if he was lucky the GP practice in his home town would be able to refer him to a nurse who specialised in the management of diabetes.

His ankle was another matter, and any decisions about that were in the hands of the orthopaedic surgeon due to arrive at any moment.

'Gwilym, how are you feeling at the moment? Is your ankle still painful?'

'What ankle?' he retorted with a grin. 'Whatever you've put in that bag of fluid is really great. I haven't felt this good in weeks. I don't even feel thirsty any more.'

'That's because we're putting water into your system at the same time as the painkillers,' she explained, knowing that was the easy part of the explanation. The next part was where she had to break the news that he'd developed a condition that was going to need daily attention to detail if he was to have a long and healthy life.

'Unfortunately,' she continued steadily, 'while we were testing your blood we discovered that there was far too much sugar in it, so we're also having to give you insulin in the drip to help your body to get rid of it.'

'Insulin?' he repeated in horror. 'But that's what you give to people with diabetes.'

'That's right,' she agreed calmly. 'When you're up on the ward and everything's back on an even keel, you'll have some more tests to find out why your body isn't getting rid of the sugar by itself.'

'So the insulin is just to sort me out at the moment, like? It won't be a permanent thing?' She could see that he really wanted her to agree, but she couldn't do that with a clear conscience, not when she knew it was so unlikely.

'I couldn't say,' she hedged, not wanting to upset him any further. 'You won't know that until you get the results of the other tests. Now,' she continued briskly when it looked as if he was going to argue the point, 'while we're waiting for the orthopaedic surgeon to come and have a look at your ankle, shall I take a quick look around the corner and see how the rest of your friends are getting on?'

'Oh, yes, please!' he agreed, easily diverted onto concerns about his friends. 'Taff especially, if you could. We were at school together when we were nippers, see, and we've lived no more than a few streets apart all our lives. We were each other's best man, too, so if anything happened to Taff, I'd have nobody left to blame...'

Maggie laughed at his dry humour. 'Well, I'll be as quick as I can. Don't run away, will you?'

'Chance would be a fine thing,' he groaned as the door swung closed behind her.

'Well, that was a bit of a damp squib,' complained one of the newer members of staff. 'I thought we were going to have a major incident to cope with, and it was mostly cuts and bruises.'

'Bite your tongue!' Lina protested disapprovingly. 'We get enough of those without wishing for them. Now you can get back to clearing the board of all the patients who've been waiting for the emergency to be over.'

Maggie paused by the board to update Gwilym's status and ran her eyes down the list of names, but couldn't see anyone called Taff.

'Lina, which ones are the other motorway crash victims? I'm looking for someone called Taff. I was treating his friend and he's worried about him.'

'Taff?' Lina laughed. 'That could apply to all of them. They're all Welshmen.'

'And all with beautiful voices,' Maggie added as several voices lifted in close harmony above the usual hubbub of the busy department. 'So it's a case of following my ears until I find the right body attached, is it?'

'More or less,' she agreed. 'Good luck.'

Maggie turned away from the board and ploughed right into a body, a big, powerful body.

'I'm so sorry,' she gasped, and tried to step back, but the owner of that big, powerful, all-too-familiar body was gripping her arms and seemed in no hurry to release her.

'I'm not sorry at all,' Jake teased. 'Feel free to

plaster yourself up against me any time you feel like it.'

'Jake!' She was startled by the innuendo in his voice and not a little flustered. He was well known for his ready charm, but until now he'd never used his familiar lines on her. 'Were you looking for something?'

'Not any more—I found it.' He wrapped an arm around her shoulders. 'Now, where were you off to in such a hurry? Can I tempt you to run away with me instead?'

'Jake, stop it!' she hissed. 'What's got into you today?'

'Spring fever, perhaps?' he suggested.

'In the middle of winter?' she scoffed. 'Be serious!'

He tucked the corners of his mouth in for all the world like a little boy trying hard to control the urge to laugh, and she had a sudden vision of their child wearing exactly the same expression of barely controlled glee.

'Well, if you've got time to lark about, I haven't,' she said severely, needing desperately to get away from him before her expression gave her away. She'd loved him for so long, and even though he hadn't acknowledged their child, every day that it grew inside her, her love for father and child was growing. 'I'm trying to find a patient called Taff so I can report back to his friend.'

'Would his friend be called Gwilym, by any chance?' If anything, Jake's grin had grown wider. 'Because, if so, I think we're on the same mission.'

'Taff wants to know how his old friend Gwilym is...'

'While Gwilym wants to know how Taff is. If that isn't a mark of true friendship...'

As if both of them had been struck by the same thought at the same time, they quickly passed on the requisite information and hurried back to their charges.

Maggie thought it was sad that neither of them had been able to meet the other's eyes while the word 'friendship' had hung in the air between them.

'Unfortunately, that's all he's ever wanted from me, while I've always wanted more...much more,' she muttered, then had to plaster on a smile before she shouldered open the doors to report back to Gwilym, in case he thought there was something seriously wrong with his friend.

'You only just got here in time, my lovely,' Gwilym pointed out amid the flurry of preparing him for transfer up to a bed in a ward. 'Did you find Taff? Have they brought him in from the crash yet?'

'Better than that, I bumped into his doctor. Taff had sent him to find out how *you* were doing.'

'So he's all right, then? Really all right?'

'I'll tell you what, how about the porters taking a slightly roundabout route to the lift so you can wave to him on your way past?' Maggie suggested. 'As I said, they're waiting for the results of some tests before they decide whether he's going to be admitted.'

'So we could end up on the same ward?' Gwilym suggested, and Maggie had to resist the urge to roll her eyes. She could just imagine the problems the staff would have with these two in the same ward. They'd probably be like two kids organising midnight feasts after lights out at boarding school.

'Not necessarily,' she warned. 'It will depend on

the sort of injuries he has. For example, because you're going to have your ankle operated on, you'll be going to Orthopaedics ward.'

'Right, we're ready to roll,' announced one of the porters, and kicked to release the brakes. 'Next stop, Resus Two, then all points north until we reach Orthopaedics.'

'Have you got time to come with us, Doctor?' Gwilym pleaded, reaching for her hand as though loath to lose the only familiar face in such a frightening environment. 'I'd like to introduce you to Taff.'

'And I'd like to meet him,' Maggie agreed. 'But I won't be able to stay long. There are a lot of people still waiting for attention. They were bumped to the back of the list when you lot came in.'

Jake was just on his way back into Resus Two when their entourage arrived.

'Are you coming to check up on me or couldn't you stay away any longer?' he teased, much to Gwilym's delight.

'Actually, we've come to see if my friend Taff's been behaving himself,' he announced chirpily. 'I was best man at his wedding, see, and I've got to keep an eye on him to make sure he doesn't stray.'

Maggie thought that there was hardly anyone less likely to stray than the pallid creature in front of her. Even when his friend tried to chivvy him into a response it was very lacklustre.

For a while she put it down to the after-effects of his excess celebrating, but a closer look at the monitors at the head of the bed told a different story, forcing her to look closer.

'Jake,' she called under cover of Gwilym's banter with the nurses, 'did you check Taff yourself?'

'No, he wasn't my patient.' He moved closer so that their conversation wouldn't alarm the subject. 'Why, Maggie? Is there a problem?'

'I just don't like the look of him. It could be something to do with the alcohol overload or the trauma of the accident, but his blood pressure's way down and he's borderline shocky. Even from here it looks as if he's got a large bruise just under his ribs at the front there. What do you think?'

Wordlessly, Jake stepped forward to cast an eagle eye over the man.

'Hello, Taff. I'm Jake Lascelles, one of the doctors. I hope you don't mind me asking, but were you thrown out of your seat in the crash?'

'Thrown out of his seat?' Gwilym hooted. 'He wasn't even in it to start with. Silly beggar was arguing with the driver about taking a...a pit stop on the hard shoulder.'

'So it's possible you might have hit yourself here when the minibus rolled over?' He rested a gentle hand over the shadowy mark on the naked belly and was rewarded with a wince out of all proportion to the pressure.

'Think I caught it on the corner of the driver's seat,' he whispered painfully. 'It aches like blazes now.'

'Large-bore cannula, please,' Jake demanded suddenly, and one of the nurses leapt to get it. 'Yellow or grey venflon, then get an oxygen mask on him and connect him up for an ECG.'

Without needing to be told, Maggie drew 20 ml of blood for cross-matching and a full blood count, and sent it off to the labs at the run. Meanwhile, Jake was running colloid in as fast as it would go in an attempt to get Taff's systolic blood pressure up closer to one hundred, but it didn't seem to be working.

'I don't think we'll waste time with a consult on this one,' Jake announced as he began disconnecting the various leads from the A and E monitoring equipment and reconnecting them immediately to a portable unit. 'Phone up and tell them he's on his way, and if they can't see him immediately…'

He didn't need to finish the sentence as Maggie reached for the phone and dialled the extension for Theatres. If Taff's hidden blood loss was greater than the flow Jake was trying to push in, she knew that the injured man couldn't afford to wait in a queue for attention—he needed it now.

The bed was on its way out of the doors by the time she finished the call.

'Mike Willson's just finished a gastric resection and is handing over the closing up to his registrar. He'll be scrubbed and ready to start as soon as you get there.'

'That's what I wanted to hear,' Jake said with a grim smile.

'Anything else you want me to do?' she offered.

'Make sure the lab knows that we need a *rapid* cross-match on that sample, and that we'll need at least four units sent straight up to Theatre. There's going to be no margin for error or delays. Oh, and explain to his friend what's happening, please,' he added just before he disappeared from view.

'What are you doing here?' Jake said, spotting Maggie sitting with a wheelchair-bound Gwilym in the most obvious place she could think of so she would see him as soon as he returned to the department.

It was only half an hour later, but it had felt like for ever while Maggie waited for news. It didn't help that Gwilym had refused to budge until he knew that his friend was going to be all right.

'What was the matter with him?' Gwilym demanded urgently. 'He's all right now, isn't he?'

'He's certainly much better than he was,' Jake confirmed. 'When the back of the driver's seat caught him amidships, it did some damage inside that meant he was losing blood. Over the space of time, it ended up being rather a lot of blood that needed replacing in a hurry.'

'But he's all right now, isn't he?' Gwilym repeated. 'It's all been fixed?'

'The surgeon told me he's pleased with his needlework, but if it hadn't been for Dr ffrench, here, spotting that Taff had been injured inside, it could have been a different story. Anyway, what are you doing down here still?' He turned to Maggie. 'Don't tell me there's a problem with finding him a bed?'

'Finding the bed wasn't the problem—it's getting the man to go up to it!' she said with a teasing smile for her companion.

'Well, I couldn't leave before I found out about Taff, could I? And Margot here has been keeping my spirits up.'

'Margot?' Jake frowned.

Maggie felt her cheeks heating and wished she'd found something else inconsequential to talk about rather than her given name.

'Dr ffrench here,' Gwilym said rather smugly.

'See, I think she's far too elegant and classy to be a Maggie, don't you?'

'Our Maggie? Elegant and classy?' Jake teased. 'Well, I must admit she does scrub up well when she's going out on the town, so perhaps you're right.'

'Well, I won't hear a word said against her,' Gwilym said stubbornly. 'Her sharp eyes saved Taff's life and…and if she ever needs a top-notch Welsh male voice choir, she only needs to say the word and we'll be there!'

CHAPTER EIGHT

'WELL spotted, Maggie!' Jake said when they managed to grab a break some time later.

'Yeah! Nice save,' said the mortified junior registrar. 'I owe you one, big time! If you hadn't spotted that shadow…' He shook his head.

'If it helps your ego, I nearly missed my first one, too,' Maggie admitted, her pleasure at Jake's praise making her generous. 'It was Jake who prompted me to look again, and the thought of what would have happened if it hadn't been picked up in time haunted me for a long time.'

'Well, I'll certainly be sharpening up my observation after today,' he agreed. 'Can I get you a coffee? Polish your shoes? Name my firstborn in your honour?'

'Just take the weight off your feet and recharge your batteries in case we get another coach party coming in,' Maggie advised. 'It's just the way things are in A and E. We all have to help each other and watch each other's backs. You'll do the same for me one day, I expect.'

'I'd be very surprised if he did,' Jake murmured, when the young man had moved away. 'You don't miss much because you're always looking and analysing, even when you're chatting to put the patient at ease. It's one of the things that makes you such a good doctor.'

Maggie was stunned into silence, totally unaccustomed to such fulsome praise from anyone, let alone someone she admired as much as Jake. Her parents certainly hadn't bothered, and her teachers had been far too impressed by David's brilliance to appreciate anything she achieved.

'It was just luck,' she said uncomfortably.

'There was no luck involved,' he denied. 'It was the result of years of hard work spent honing your skills, and today was one of the special days when you actually see it paying off.'

'Special days?'

'Exactly,' he said firmly. 'Most shifts, whether they're manic or boring, are composed of bread-and-butter medicine that you see day in and day out—the heart attacks and strokes, the broken bones and lacerations, the drug overdoses and suicides. Each time it's a one-of-a-kind crisis to the patient but just more of the same for us, with the odd variation thrown in to keep us on our toes. But every so often there'll be something that you spot—sometimes it's so insignificant that it could all too easily be overlooked in the frantic pace of a busy shift—'

'Like the shadow of a blow to the abdomen?'

'Precisely! And you'll go home tonight knowing that you absolutely, unquestionably played your part in saving someone from certain death. And I guarantee,' he added, 'that those are the cases that stick with you and make you want to keep on doing the job even when you're so tired you can hardly see straight.'

'So, tell me about one of yours,' she challenged, relishing the return to their former ease with each other. Soon they would have to go their separate ways to finish their shift, but for now they were just two friends sharing thoughts and feelings about something that meant a great deal to both of them—their profession.

'Her name was Holly Hunter,' he said with a reminiscent smile.

'What? The film star?' Maggie gasped.

'No!' He chuckled. 'This was the *other* Holly Hunter—a stunning redhead and an absolute charmer of a four-year-old.'

Maggie's laughter was rather more ragged than she would have wished as she was fighting the grip of jealousy around her throat right up to the moment he'd mentioned the patient's age.

'And? What was wrong with her?' she prompted.

'Epilepsy, apparently, and the fits were growing more frequent in spite of medication.'

'So, what did you see?' Maggie demanded, her brain already sifting through dozens of possible scenarios while he kept her hanging—everything from allergies to drug reactions to head trauma.

'Her eye was different,' he said cryptically, but it was enough to put her on the right track.

'Bulging eye or deviation?' she demanded. 'Was it a tumour? A glioma, perhaps?'

He smiled broadly and that was enough reward for her.

'Yes, the epilepsy was being triggered by a tumour and the size of it—about the size of a hen's egg— was starting to make her eye bulge out, but it was a meningioma rather than a glioma.'

'Meningioma? Wow! That's rare in a four-year-old. Onset is more common in middle age, isn't it?'

'Precisely. But on the other hand it was extremely

lucky, because gliomas at that age are often aggressively malignant while the meningioma was benign.'

'But it wouldn't have to be malignant to kill her,' Maggie pointed out. 'Just the increasing pressure as it continued to grow would eventually have destroyed her brain.'

'As it is, thanks to a very brave neurosurgeon there was a happy ending. She's now in senior school and hoping to go on to train as a doctor. Her mother sent me a card not long ago because she thought I'd like to know.'

'Jake?' Lina's voice hailed him from the doorway. 'We've got a little girl *en route* in an ambulance. She's fitting badly and none of the usual medication seems to be helping. ETA four minutes.'

'Oh, that's a spooky coincidence.' Maggie shuddered. 'Still, it was time we got back to work anyway. Good luck with the little girl.'

'Thanks. See you later. Don't forget that we're going out tonight, will you?'

Maggie blinked at the reminder, her gaze on the busy-shift-rumpled green cotton draped over the most grabbable male backside, riveted until the door swung closed and cut off the enticing view.

She blinked again to clear her thoughts, because she *had* forgotten that he'd asked her to join him for a meal out, and then she groaned, afraid that she wasn't going to be able to think of anything else *but* Jake and his invitation for the rest of the day.

She was right.

When she was cleaning up a particularly messy gash on an elderly woman's hand, and having to use steri-strips to hold it together because the skin was too fine and tissue-paper thin to tolerate stitches, she was trying to remember whether she'd brought her smarter trousers with her to change into after work.

When she was irrigating a carpenter's eyes in an attempt to remove a huge quantity of sawdust, she was wondering exactly where Jake intended taking her, and while she was waiting for the ultrasound technician to scan a woman afraid she'd just lost her precious baby, she found herself wondering why he'd asked her out in the first place.

For heaven's sake, they were sharing space at his flat and they worked together—did they really need to spend any more time together? It was hard enough trying to keep her thoughts and feelings under control without the added risk of spending time in a social setting. There was too much chance that she would reveal the direction of those thoughts and feelings and put a destructive strain on their newly restored friendship.

Unfortunately, the only alternative she could think of was to stay busy. But as Jake was also her superior he was in a position to know when she was volunteering for extra work and he was intelligent enough to work out why.

'Anyway, it's too late to do anything about it tonight,' she muttered as she bent over the ubiquitous mountain of paperwork, making sure that she'd signed off on the treatment she'd performed on each of her patients. 'I'll just have to grin and bear it.'

Even as she said the words, she felt guilty. They made her sound so ungrateful when he'd been considerate enough to offer to take her out.

The trouble was, she really wanted to spend time with him, the way any woman wanted to spend time with the man she loved, but the sane part of her mind knew that it would only lead to heartache. Her heart was already aching in spite of the fact that she was carrying his baby, because she knew it was a child he'd never wanted and it was being carried by a woman he didn't love.

So, where did that leave her? she thought as she grabbed a quick shower at the end of her shift, once more having to fight the images of what had happened on the fateful night that she and Jake had shared a shower.

She loved the man and he'd offered to marry her, that was fact number one, but she could hardly delude herself into thinking it was love that had prompted the proposal. That led her to fact number two, that even though she knew he didn't love her she was tempted to accept—to take what she could get and hope it would be enough.

Except there was fact number three, her deepest, darkest secret.

It had taken her years before she'd realised her biggest flaw, and it was one that would guarantee that their union could never last. It wouldn't matter what she did or how hard she tried, he would never love her because nobody did, not even her mother.

'Are you in there, Maggie?' The sudden demand was accompanied by a thump on the outer door, Jake's voice catapulting her out of her thoughts. 'Hurry up! I'm starving to death out here!'

For just one cowardly moment she contemplated ignoring him in the hope that he would go away, but deep down she knew that wasn't her style. All her life she'd been a fighter, first when she'd tried to compete with David for their parents' attention and then when she'd embarked on one of the most demanding of all the hospital specialties—emergency medicine.

'I won't be long!' she called back. 'Go and gnaw on a chair leg for a minute.' She quickly scrubbed a towel over herself and dragged clean underwear on over her damp skin, all the while giving herself a stern lecture.

'So you're in love with the man. So what? He's not responsible for your feelings. So he proposed...or rather, offered to marry you. You knew he didn't love you the way you need to be loved, so you turned him down.' Turned him down even though she'd wanted to shriek her acceptance and drag him off to do it before he came to his senses.

'So tonight you're going to share a meal with him and you're going to be your usual sane and sensible self. If he proposes again you're going to politely turn him down again and tell him that you wouldn't dream of tying him to someone he didn't love, and then you're going to sanely and sensibly ask him what he wants to do about visitation rights and—'

'Maggie!' There was a despairing tone to his voice this time that made her wonder just how long she'd been standing there rabbiting on about what she was going to do instead of getting on with it.

She took one last glance in the mirror at the inexpensive black jeans topped by a cream cowl necked jumper and grimaced at the neat, plain, boring, totally unlovable individual looking back at her, then reached for the door.

'I'm ready!' she announced, automatically turning towards the exit nearest the staff car park, only pausing when she realised that Jake wasn't following.

She turned back to find out what was the matter,

to discover he was still leaning against the wall with a slightly bemused expression on his face.

'What are you waiting for?' she demanded, uncomfortable when she realised that those dark blue eyes were scanning her from head to toe.

One quick glance at him was enough to tell her that he looked as devastating as ever, his beloved disreputable-looking leather jacket giving him that irresistible 'bad boy' air that went with tousled dark hair and a chiselled jaw shadowed by his emerging beard. Her fingers tingled with the memory of the sound it made as she'd explored that roughness in the middle of the night, and she was so preoccupied that she nearly missed his words.

'I wanted to give you this,' he said diffidently, holding out one of the flowers that were sold in the concession stand in the hospital's main reception area.

It was a rose. A red rose.

Her heart gave a swift double beat before settling into a faster pace than usual.

'For me?' she whispered, not certain that she could manage any more than that without any breath.

He shrugged, looking uncharacteristically uncomfortable. 'I just thought... I wanted to... It's a sort of a "congratulations" in honour of your sharp eyes this afternoon,' he finished in a hurry, sounding almost as if he was wishing he hadn't bothered.

Maggie was torn between joy that he'd thought to give her a flower at all and disappointment that he'd chosen the traditional symbol of love. For one stupid, crazy moment, she'd actually thought he was going to say...what? That he'd had a blinding flash of revelation and was madly in love with her?

Ha! Dream on! That sort of thing only happened

in the sort of films made when her grandmother had been alive.

'Thank you, Jake,' she murmured belatedly, cradling the blossom tenderly. 'You didn't have to do this. I was only doing my job.'

'You never *only* do your job,' he contradicted, gesturing for her to start walking towards the exit before he continued. 'Right from the first I saw that you threw yourself into A and E medicine heart and soul, as if every patient really meant something to you. I suppose that's one of the reasons why we became friends—because we have a similar attitude.'

Maggie was secretly thrilled by his praise. She knew that they worked well together, but to know that he valued her so highly almost made up for the fact that was their only relationship.

'Except, unlike you, I never intended my profession to be my whole life,' she argued, deliberately pointing out the essential difference between the two of them to keep her feet on the ground. 'I'd always hoped that I would have, well, in the usual phrase… "have it all"—the absorbing job *and* the loving husband and family.'

She could have kicked herself when her words fell into an uncomfortable silence. She'd only been rehashing an oft-rehearsed argument between them, but this time it had a completely different connotation. This time there was the fact that they'd spent the night together and created a baby. This time there was the fact that he'd mentioned the forbidden word… 'marriage'.

'So, how is Taff? Have you heard?' she asked brightly, but wincing inside at the abrupt change of topic.

'The man must have the constitution of an ox.' Jake laughed, apparently willing to go along with it. 'Not only did he survive emergency surgery with far less than a full quota of blood, but when he came round he didn't even have the grace to suffer from a hangover. Then, in spite of the fact that his guts are held together with stitches and staples, he starts serenading the nurse supposed to be specialling him with a romantic ballad in Welsh!'

'I've heard that they breed them tough in the valleys.' Maggie chuckled, almost more in relief than in appreciation of the humour in the situation. At least they wouldn't be getting indigestion from eating a meal in a heavy atmosphere.

Jake breathed a sigh that combined relief and frustration as he collapsed back onto his pillow that night.

The relief was that, after a few sticky moments at the beginning of the evening when he'd nearly tripped over his tongue at the sight and scent of a freshly showered Maggie, slim and sexy in black jeans but temptingly cuddly-looking in a top that tempted him to touch, they'd managed to revert to their usual mixture of light-hearted banter and serious discussion about every topic under the sun.

Every topic, that was, except the one he wanted to discuss—the fact that she'd turned down his offer of marriage. He needed to know why before he could tell whether he had a chance to change her mind. After all, she was pregnant. She was going to need someone to help share the load and, by proposing, he'd indicated he was willing, so why had she dismissed the idea out of hand?

'Still, she *had* made the effort to look nice before

we went out,' he murmured in consolation to his bruised ego, the image of her slender elegance in nothing more sophisticated than a pair of jeans and a pale top enough to start his pulse pounding all over again. 'That must mean something. And as for her reaction to the flower...'

He wondered if it had been the right gesture to make, knowing that roses had a special significance, and red roses in particular.

'But, dammit, I *do* love her, so why shouldn't I give her a red rose?' Then he pulled a face. 'Except I should have been able to say the words when I gave it to her, and I can't because she wouldn't want to hear them. Not from me.'

He remembered just how hard it had been not to blurt them out when they'd been making love. Only the thought that it would destroy everything between them had helped him to bite his tongue.

'One day,' he said softly, determined to do everything he could to try to persuade her to accept his offer, even if he had to play on the fact that his financial situation could make life easier for both Maggie and the baby. But he'd rather not do that if he didn't have to. He'd rather see if he could build on the strength of their friendship and turn it into the firm foundations of a love to last a lifetime.

The trouble was, everything in him wanted to charge at the situation at a full gallop. In the dark privacy of his room he could admit that he was afraid that if she had too much time to think she would realise just how bad a bargain she was getting... especially once she learned his secret.

It seemed wrong that he should be trying to win her affection without putting all his cards on the table from the beginning, but he knew at first hand what a difference that could make.

Twice he'd been up-front with women when he'd realised he was growing serious about the relationship, and both times it had signalled an ignominious end. This time he was playing his cards close to his chest and ignoring his conscience until there was a chance that Maggie wouldn't care about his problem.

'Where is Maggie? I thought she was on duty today?'

Maggie grimaced when she heard Jake's voice outside in the corridor. The last couple of weeks it seemed as if she could hardly turn round without bumping into him. The female staff washroom was probably the only place left where he couldn't track her down.

Not that she wanted to spend the rest of her life there, although that seemed a definite option today, with violent nausea striking her every few minutes.

She didn't hear her colleague's reply but Jake's 'Well, will you page her for me, please? She's got a phone call' sounded abrupt and much less than conciliatory.

Sure enough, the infernal pager clipped to her pocket sounded its shrill demand within seconds and she groaned, hoping she would actually be able to leave the room for long enough to find out who was calling her and why it had put Jake in such a bad mood.

She wiped her mouth with a tissue and stood up, only then remembering that recently her bladder seemed to have shrunk to the capacity of a child's thimble. Today her stomach was aching, too, the way it had after she'd made the mistake of signing up for the intermediate exercise class at the gym. Was that another of the delightful results of all the retching she'd been doing?

'God must have been a man,' she muttered grimly. 'A woman definitely wouldn't have made pregnancy so awful.' She turned to flush the toilet and couldn't believe her eyes.

'I'm bleeding,' she gasped, her hand flying protectively to her stomach as though that would stop anything happening to her precious baby.

'Maggie? Are you in there?' This time there was concern in Jake's voice as he rapped on the door. 'Are you all right?'

'Oh, Jake!' she whimpered, needing him more than she could say.

'I'm coming in, Maggie,' he warned, and she nearly laughed out loud.

How like him to charge into a situation himself rather than send a female member of staff in his place. She heard the sound of the door opening and his footsteps coming closer.

'Maggie? Are you here?'

'Yes, Jake.' She fumbled with the lock, her knees suddenly threatening to let her down. 'I'm here. Please… Please.'

She didn't know what she was pleading for, but in her shocked state all she knew was that Jake would be able to give it to her.

'What's the matter? Aren't you feeling well?' he demanded as soon as he caught sight of her.

Silently, she gestured towards the toilet, unable to look at the evidence again. She knew exactly when he registered what he was seeing by the expression of distress on his face.

'Fetch a wheelchair,' he demanded abruptly, throwing the request over his shoulder towards the gaggle of interested bodies grouped around the doorway even as he wrapped a supportive arm around her shoulders.

'Better yet, make that a trolley,' he amended, probably prompted by the fact that she was almost a dead weight against him. 'And the rest of you can get back to work. This isn't a circus sideshow.'

Maggie was barely aware of the avid eyes and couldn't have cared less about anything other than the fact that Jake had come when she needed him and he would take care of her. Jake would do everything he could for her and their baby.

It didn't seem in the least bit strange that he should sweep her up off her feet and into his arms, or that he seemed reluctant to put her on the trolley when it arrived. It seemed perfectly natural that he should be holding tightly to her hand even as he barked orders at the hapless orderlies to get her into the nearest resus room.

Almost before she knew what was happening, she found herself flat on her back with her feet raised, an oxygen mask over her face and an IV line being expertly inserted and taped into position.

'Hey!' she objected, but nobody was listening to her muffled voice. Anyway, they were too busy trying to keep up with Jake's rapid-fire orders.

She reached the end of her limited patience when she saw the all-too-familiar scissors descending towards her clothing.

'No way!' Maggie yelped, startling the stuffing out of the junior nurse by grabbing her hand before the poor girl could make the first cut. She might be flattered beyond belief that he was so concerned about her, but there was no way she was going to be stripped naked in front of a room full of her colleagues.

'Jake!' she shouted, then dragged the stifling mask off her face to shout again. 'Jake Lascelles! Will you *stop* this? It's unnecessary!' To say nothing of being embarrassing beyond belief, knowing that she was going to be the hot item of gossip for the whole hospital yet again.

This time he heard her, whirling round and bending over her anxiously.

'What's the matter, Maggie? Are you in pain?'

'No. But *you* will be if you don't stop this!' she hissed through gritted teeth.

'But, Maggie—'

'But nothing!' she snapped. 'I would like a word with you, please…in private!'

'But…' For one of the few times that she could remember in an A and E situation, Jake looked uncertain and it was rather endearing. But, endearing or not, she couldn't let him steamroller her any more. She glared at him and he actually backed down.

'OK. You heard her,' he grumbled. 'Find something else to do for a couple of minutes—but don't go far.'

From the expression on some of the departing faces Maggie hadn't a doubt that there would be more than a few of them loitering nearby in the hope of picking up something juicy to pass on, but there was little she could do about that. To insist they withdraw to the other end of the corridor would be overkill and only draw more attention to herself.

'Maggie—'

'Damn you, Jake!' she muttered, close to tears.

'Why didn't you order up a brass band while you were about it?'

'What?' Now he was totally bewildered.

'Oh, for heaven's sake!' she exploded, then forced herself to lower her voice before she continued. 'You were the only person I'd told about the baby, but now the whole world will know that I was pregnant. All you needed to do was help me to one of the cubicles and do an ultrasound. No one would have been any the wiser.'

'Oh, God, Maggie, I'm sorry,' he said, clearly stricken. 'When I saw the blood, all I could think about was taking you somewhere I could look after you. I didn't think about the fact that it would mean everybody would get to know about the baby.'

'Well, it's done now,' she said wearily, the fact of her loss suddenly hitting her with devastating force. What she wanted to do was find somewhere totally private where she could pull the covers up over her head and cry for all her broken dreams. But first there was the final test to perform, to confirm what had happened.

'Jake, forget it. All you need to do is get a technician in to confirm what's happened. No doubt there'll be something else along in a day or two to take my name out of the gossip headlines.'

'I'll do it myself,' he said softly, and the misery in his blue gaze was almost enough to break her control. She hadn't realised that Jake, the man who'd said he didn't want to have wife or family, would be so upset about losing something he'd never wanted.

Or had he changed his mind? Had the knowledge that he'd fathered a child had such a profound effect on him that he would genuinely mourn its loss?

In silence, she watched as he prepared the high-tech machinery, only moving when it was time to bare her ominously concave belly to the chill of the conductive jelly.

She couldn't bear to see the evidence that she'd lost the tiny life inside her, guilt like a huge dark cloud surrounding her.

'Jake, could it be my fault?' she whispered through a throat tight with the threat of tears. 'We always follow safety protocol when X-rays are taken, but could I have forgotten? It was weeks before I realised that I was pregnant. Could a dose of radiation have caused birth abnormalities that made my body reject the baby?'

Jake paused long enough in his preparations to cup her cheek in his palm, directing her gaze to meet his.

'Maggie, don't do this to yourself,' he said sternly. 'Knowing how much you want a family, do you honestly think you would have forgotten to protect your ovaries?' He closed his eyes for a moment and sighed before continuing. 'You know as well as I do that it's actually the minority of pregnancies that go to full term without a hitch. The vast majority are lost before the twelve-week mark, most of them without the mothers even being certain they were pregnant. It's just one of those things, and most women go on to have perfectly healthy children the next time they try.'

But it won't be *your* baby, she thought in anguish, stunned by the realisation that the thought of carrying anyone else's baby felt completely wrong. With the icy calm of inevitability she knew that if the baby had gone she'd just lost her only chance at the family she'd always wanted.

CHAPTER NINE

'HAVE you had any other bleeds or spotting so far?' Jake asked, apparently reverting completely to calm professionalism as he began to pass the probe across her skin. This time she couldn't force herself to look away as it picked up the shadowy reflected images and transmitted them to the screen.

'No. Well, yes, I suppose I must have...at least once,' she contradicted herself immediately. 'Maybe twice—otherwise I would have realised I was pregnant much sooner.'

'So you might just be one of those women who have a "show" for the first couple of months when their period would normally have been due?'

'I suppose,' she agreed distractedly as she twisted her head around in an attempt to get a clearer view of the screen.

'I'm sorry it's taking so long,' he apologised as he pressed switches on the state-of-the-art console. The equipment was some of the newest, that combined traditional ultrasound scanning with the facility for continuous monitoring of the heartbeat of both mother and baby. 'I don't usually get my hands on this bit of kit—well, there isn't usually time for me to do it and—'

Maggie gasped.

She barely noticed that Jake had stopped speaking because she stopped breathing altogether when she saw the blob on the screen suddenly resolve itself into a recognisable shape.

Was it just wishful thinking or was that really the rapid flickering of a tiny beating heart?

With a sudden imprecation Jake did something else to the controls and for the first time she heard the sound of her baby's heart.

'Oh, Jake,' she whispered, tears beginning to trickle down her cheeks. She placed a protective hand over her belly, marvelling at the invisible miracle inside. 'It's still there.'

'It certainly is,' he said gruffly, as if he was having trouble speaking, too. He pressed a few more buttons to set the printer whining into life, and under Maggie's fascinated gaze the image on the screen was reproduced on paper. 'I've recorded the scan, too,' he told her, the words floating over her head for a moment until she forced herself to pay attention.

'Recorded it? Why? Is there a problem?' The words were almost tumbling over each other because she was trying to get the questions out so fast, but not nearly as fast as her accelerating pulse with the thought that there was something wrong with her precious baby.

'Calm down, Maggie, and give me a chance to finish,' he said, gripping her icy hand in the warmth of his. 'As far as I can tell, everything's absolutely normal, but I don't see very many of these, so I just wanted to be certain. Is Dan Freeman your gynae?'

She nodded shakily, feeling more like a disjointed puppet than a calm, controlled A and E registrar. 'I haven't seen him yet, but I've made an appointment for later on this week.'

'Well, Dan will be able to reassure you that everything's OK as soon as he's seen the recording.'

'When?' she demanded frantically, all her protective instincts aroused. 'I won't have to wait until my appointment, will I?'

'I don't know, but I'll find out,' he promised, his usual decisiveness sharpened by something that seemed far more personal.

'Here.' He offered her a handful of paper tissues to wipe off the stickiness of the jelly. 'You clean yourself up while I see what I can do. Oh, and here's something for you to be looking at in the meantime.' He reached down to the printer tray and extracted the single sheet of paper lying there.

Maggie's free hand was shaking as she reached out to take it and the paper was trembling so much that she could barely focus on the image it contained.

'Thank you, Jake,' she breathed, dragging her eyes away long enough to look up at him. 'Thank you for…for everything.'

'You're entirely welcome, Maggie ffrench,' he said with a brief smile before turning towards the phone.

Suddenly she remembered that their every word was probably being monitored by half a department.

'Jake, before you do that, should you make sure you haven't still got everyone out in the corridor waiting around to hear their master's voice?'

He pulled a face at her. 'I suppose there are some real patients they could be attending to,' he conceded, diverting his steps towards the door. 'But Lina probably collared them and put them to work ages ago.'

She tuned out his conversation as his call was put through to the department almost at the top of the building, focusing all her attention on an image that wouldn't have looked out of place as a Rorschach ink blot.

He must have called in a few favours, because when he turned back to her he was wearing a smile.

'Dan's on his way down as we speak,' he announced triumphantly. 'I always knew they didn't have enough to do up there. Can you imagine someone from A and E being able to abandon everything at the drop of a hat and go gallivanting around the hospital?'

'No,' she agreed with choked laughter. 'They just commandeer half of the staff and turn a run-of-the-mill obstetric incident into a major trauma.'

'I didn't!' he objected, and when she merely raised an eloquent eyebrow he conceded, 'Well, you could have been haemorrhaging to death. I had to make sure that—'

'Jake,' she interrupted, holding up her hand to stem his explanation, her heart suddenly light enough to float. He might not have said anything, but his swift actions had certainly proved his concern for the child he'd fathered. 'I'm not really complaining—except about nearly ending up naked on the trolley. I just wanted to say thank you for being such a good friend, for caring that our—'

'Right, mate,' Dan said as he breezed into the room. 'Where's this dodgy movie you want to show me? Has the vice squad been informed? Oops! My apologies, Maggie. Jake didn't say it was you…er, that the two of you were, er…'

'Quit while you're ahead,' Jake advised, and gestured towards the waiting equipment. 'I think I managed to work out how the thing records a scan, but—'

Dan waved dismissively. 'These things are made

for idiots to be able to use—but of course they work far better in the hands of highly skilled people such as myself. All I need to do is… Ah, here we go!' He leaned forward, gazing intently at the screen, and Maggie's eyes were once more riveted to a rerun of the magic moment when she'd seen that her baby—their baby—was still alive.

Dan was muttering under his breath as he played the recording several times, pausing the run twice for a closer look.

Maggie wondered if she was the only one who could feel the tension rising until Jake's hand sought hers and gripped tight.

'Well,' Dan said as he straightened up and turned to face them. 'As you saw, I did my best, but I can't tell yet which one of you the poor child's going to take after. At least the basic development appears to be going perfectly normally.'

'Oh, but it isn't—' Jake began, but Maggie cut him off, too impatient to wait while he prevaricated to divert the hospital grapevine. As concerned as he'd been for the baby's survival, she just didn't understand why he wasn't willing to openly admit he was the father.

'Are you certain?' she demanded, swinging her legs over the side so that she could sit up properly, then tucking the modesty blanket firmly around her. She'd been feeling at a decided disadvantage, lying down while everyone else was standing. 'I know that a huge proportion of spontaneous abortions and near misses are because there's something wrong with the embryo—that the mother's body somehow knows and wants to get rid of it to start afresh. Can you be sure that this wasn't…?'

'Saints preserve me from patients with medical qualifications!' Dan exclaimed with a theatrical roll of his eyes. 'They're always looking for trouble.'

'But—'

'Listen, Maggie,' he interrupted seriously, all trace of his former light-hearted banter gone as he made his point, 'I promise you that I've looked very carefully and everything seems to be perfectly normal, but if it'll make you feel happier I'll book you in for a repeat scan in another month, when the little creature will be a bit easier to see. We might even be able to tell the sex by then, if he or she is in an obliging mood.'

'I don't care what sex it is, just as long as it's healthy,' she said fervently, finally allowing herself to relax a little. 'And I can't thank you enough for coming down so quickly. I would probably have ended up on the psychiatric ward if I'd had to wait until my regular appointment.'

'Well, now you know everything's OK you can really start enjoying all the delights of losing your breakfast and increasingly frequent urination. If you're at all worried, don't hesitate to buzz for me. Other than that, I'll expect to see your name in my appointment book at regular intervals to keep a check on progress, but by the time you forget what your feet look like you'll wonder why you were so keen to have the little blighter in the first place!'

His big understanding grin told her he was only joking as he waved them both farewell, leaving the room seeming strangely quiet, yet full of the echoes of what might have happened, which were only kept at bay by Jake's reassuring presence.

'Right, Maggie,' he said heartily, giving her hand

a final squeeze before he released it, leaving her feeling somehow abandoned, 'I'd like to admit you for a couple of days' observation, just to make sure that—'

'What are you talking about?' she demanded. 'You just heard Dan. He doesn't want to see me until I book in for my routine antenatal visit. He certainly didn't suggest admitting me.'

'But—'

'But nothing!' she said firmly, clutching the blanket at her waist to preserve her modesty as she slid her feet to the floor. 'He's the specialist in his field and he knows what he's talking about.'

'OK,' Jake conceded. 'But you've had a bad scare today, and as it's only a matter or an hour or so until the end of your shift will you humour me by agreeing to go home early?'

Silently Maggie had to agree with him that she probably wasn't fit to work at the moment, so it wasn't difficult to agree to his compromise.

'I'll get my things. Do you know what's happened to my shoes? I need to get to my locker to change my clothes, and I'll need to find some more underwear.'

Jake choked at the final announcement, and before he turned away she could have sworn that he'd actually been blushing at the reminder that she'd been sitting there with her lower half covered by nothing more than a blanket.

'I'll organise a taxi for you,' he said gruffly as he made for the door. 'No point in leaving anything to chance, just in case you feel wobbly.'

'How can I help loving him?' she whispered, her heart melting at his thoughtfulness. If only he could love her in return...

*   *   *

'Hey, Maggie!' called one of the nurses by the main reception desk a short while later. 'Did you get your message?'

'Message?' She detoured towards the desk. 'What message?'

'It was a man with a gorgeous deep voice. He said he was your brother but, then, they all say that, don't they?' she teased slyly.

'What was his name? David?' Maggie demanded, simultaneously cross that she'd missed his call and worried about why he was ringing her in the first place. The cost of long-distance calls from New Zealand to England had quickly prompted them to change to e-mails for their regular means of communication, with the telephone reserved for anything more urgent or special, such as birthdays or Christmas.

'Yes, it *was* someone called David,' she admitted, pulling a disappointed face that it really had been her brother. 'When we couldn't track you down, he said he'd call back in a couple of hours.' She glanced at the big clock up on the wall. 'That'll be in about ten minutes or so.'

It was Maggie's turn to pull a face. She had a taxi waiting, and now that the terror-induced adrenaline rush of thinking she was losing her baby had faded, she just wanted to collapse in a heap, preferably in her bed. She certainly didn't want to hang around here, waiting for a phone call.

The decision was simple.

'When he calls, could you give him another number for me, please?' She accepted the pen and piece of paper the young woman offered with a smile and quickly scribbled down Jake's phone number. 'Thank you so much for being messenger. He lives in New Zealand and I haven't seen him for ages, so I really don't want to miss him. I should be at this number in about ten minutes but could you tell him to give me a bit of leeway for traffic?'

She was still worried about why David was phoning, but somehow just the thought that she'd be talking to him in the next half-hour lent an extra spring to her step as she hurried out towards the waiting taxi. In spite of the fact that her parents had unfairly favoured him she'd always loved her big brother, and she missed him now that he was living on the other side of the world.

Jake paused outside his front door to scrub both hands over his face.

He was certain that he'd aged at least ten years when he'd caught sight of Maggie clinging to the frame of the toilet cubicle, her face with all the colour and substance of skimmed milk. Then, when he'd seen what had taken the strength out of her limbs, the impact had rivalled at least a five on the Richter scale.

When she'd first told him that she was pregnant he'd been desperately jealous, certain that she would soon be out of his life for good. It had been bad enough when she'd been going to marry his long-time friend. But at least he'd known that she would still be working with him and he wouldn't lose her as a friend.

Her pregnancy had somehow seemed more…final. Knowing she'd always wanted to be a wife and mother, he knew she would willingly give up work while her baby was small.

Then, when there had been no mention of the

baby's father, and Maggie had seemed as if she was just going to continue working as though nothing had changed, he'd wondered if this might be his chance. If she was going to have the traditional stable family she'd always wanted, would she accept him as an integral part of the unit, in spite of the fact he'd been at such great pains to keep his distance over the last two years?

Today it had seemed as if he was finally making some progress, even though it had taken something as traumatic as the apparent loss of her baby to have her turning to him.

He flexed his hand, remembering the fervent way she'd clung to it while they'd waited for Dan to examine the recording of the scan. She'd had no way of knowing, but his heart had been pounding as hard as if it had been *his* child they were looking at on the screen, and when Dan had given the all-clear he'd had to fight back tears every bit as much as she had.

He drew in a steadying breath, needing to be certain that he had his emotions under control before he came face to face with her again. Hopefully she would already be asleep and he wouldn't see her until the morning, but—

A sudden peal of laughter cut his thoughts dead. He would know that merry sound anywhere, but he certainly hadn't thought to hear it coming out of his flat tonight.

Had something happened? Was it laughter or was Maggie hysterical? Had she miscarried after all?

His hands were shaking so hard he could hardly force the key into the lock, question after question tumbling around in his head.

Finally the catch released and he stumbled into the

flat just in time to see Maggie fling herself into the open arms of a complete stranger.

'Oh, I have missed you!' she exclaimed, obviously completely oblivious to Jake's presence in the flat. 'Why didn't you tell me you were coming? How long can you stay?'

A fist tightened around his heart when he saw the love shining out of her face. She was almost incandescent with it in a way he'd never seen before, and her spirits were as bright and bubbly as the first time he'd met her—the day he'd fallen head over heels in love with her.

He cleared his throat.

'I hope I'm not interrupting anything,' he said sarcastically, but his tone seemed to sail right over head.

'Oh, Jake, don't be silly!' She giggled, almost dancing as she came across and took his arm to drag him into the room. 'Come in! Of course you're not interrupting. Well, it wouldn't matter if you were, because it's your flat after all!'

Her companion was a different matter, his expression darkly drawn in spite of the deep tan and sunbleached streaks in his hair. He certainly didn't seem pleased to see Maggie's flatmate return.

'I got his message just as I was leaving the hospital but I thought he was going to phone me,' Maggie continued irrepressibly, apparently not even noticing the black scowls the two men in the room were exchanging. 'I didn't think for one minute he'd be here in person. Isn't it great? Shall I put the kettle on? Then we can all sit down.'

Jake didn't know whether to laugh or cry to see Maggie this animated about the man's arrival. If he hadn't known better, he'd have thought she was as high as a kite on something illegal. She'd certainly never been this pleased to see *him*.

'You sit down with your visitor,' he suggested, needing a little space to get his shredded emotions under control. 'I'll make the tea. Have you had anything to eat since you came home?'

'Not yet. As soon as he phoned to say he was coming I put one of my lasagnes into the oven and some potatoes into the microwave to bake. I was going to prepare a salad to go with it.' She bounced straight up out of her seat again.

'Maggie, sit!' he ordered exasperatedly. 'I'm perfectly capable of making a pot of tea and a salad!'

For the first time Maggie's guest smiled, and Jake suddenly recognised the likeness between them.

'You're David, aren't you?' he said, almost sick with relief as the tight knots started unravelling inside his chest and his heart began beating properly.

'Of *course* it's David!' Maggie exclaimed. 'I introduced you to him, remember?'

'Actually, you didn't, Moggie,' David said with a grin, finally offering his hand to Jake in a friendly greeting. 'You were too busy rattling on nineteen to the dozen and not making a lot of sense with any of it. It's good to see that Jake has learned how to get through to you.'

'What do you mean?' she demanded suspiciously, looking from one to the other as Jake returned the grin.

'"Maggie, *sit*!"' David mimicked. 'Just treat you like an exuberant puppy and you'll soon come to heel! Oof!' he exclaimed when Maggie flung a cushion at him in retaliation.

'Moggie?' Jake questioned, wondering if he'd heard David right.

Maggie pulled a face and David laughed. 'It was my nickname for her when she was younger. Our parents didn't like her to be called Maggie and she hated being called Margot and both of them hated me calling her Moggie!'

After the tensions of the day, it was a relief to spend a leisurely hour over Maggie's excellent cooking while listening to tales of the exploits she had undertaken in her quest to attract her parents' attention.

'They were lucky you stuck to the right side of the law,' Jake commented quietly at one point. 'Some kids don't.'

'I wouldn't have dared,' Maggie admitted candidly, with a glance towards the big brother she clearly adored in spite of the problems his existence had caused in her life. 'Mother and Father probably wouldn't have noticed even if I'd ended up behind bars with a criminal record, but I didn't want to disappoint David. I just wanted to beat him at his own game.'

'How she ever thought she was going to go undetected in the middle of a rugby squad, I don't know.' David shook his head, going back to one of her more notable attempts at emulating his own successes. 'And the crazy thing is that she actually scored a try, because the opposing team was so gob-smacked to see those long legs in a pair of skimpy shorts that they were tripping all over each other rather than trying to catch her before she carried the ball over the line.'

His laughter was cut short by an enormous yawn.

'Sorry about that, but I think I left my brain somewhere over the Pacific and my body hasn't got a clue what time of day it's supposed to be. I'd better find myself a room in a hotel before I fall asleep in the gutter somewhere.'

'You don't need to go to a hotel—does he, Jake?' She turned to him with a pleading expression. 'He could stay here, couldn't he?'

The suggestion caught Jake on the hop, but it was obvious what Maggie wanted him to say.

'Of course he can.' He shrugged. 'One more won't make any difference.'

'I certainly won't be awake in time to fight you for the bathroom,' David promised around another enormous yawn. 'Just point me in the right direction for the nearest horizontal surface.'

Jake sat still, hardly daring to breathe while he waited to see what arrangements Maggie was going to make for the night.

The fact that she settled her brother into the spare room she'd been using was an obvious move, but with her brother in her bed, where was *she* intending to sleep?

They both knew that although his settee was perfectly comfortable for a doze in front of the television, it would probably cause permanent spinal damage to anyone trying to sleep on it for a complete night. Of course if he were a gentleman he would offer to sleep on it, or even to sleep on the floor, so that she could have his bed.

Unfortunately, where Maggie was concerned, he was far too selfish to be a gentleman any more. His recent scare, thinking that David was the father of her baby come to take her away, had finally brought him to his senses. It was all very well playing a waiting game in the hope that she was going to fall in love with him, but that seemed to be causing more problems than it was solving. Anyway, it went against his years of training not to take charge of a situation if there was something he could do.

He closed his eyes and focused on one basic fact— the core reason for his entire existence ever since he'd met her—his love for Maggie ffrench. Suddenly he knew what he was going to have to do. He didn't have any option if he was going to stay sane because the uncertainty couldn't go on any longer.

'So, that's it,' he muttered, jackknifing out of the chair and beginning to pace backwards and forwards like a caged beast in the confines of his compact living room. There was no way he could sit still with so much hanging on the outcome of the next few minutes.

'As soon as she comes back from organising her brother, I'm going to sit her down and put all my cards on the table,' he muttered, trying to build up his determination in spite of his fear of failure and the temptation to leave things as they were. After all, having Maggie as a friend was better than nothing, and if—

'No!' He closed his eyes and took a calming breath. 'After two years of believing she was permanently out of my reach, the situation has changed. She's pregnant, and apparently alone, and I know she believes that children are better off with two parents.' He paused, overwhelmed for a moment by the image of the two of them cradling her child between them. Would it ever come true?

'You won't know unless you try,' he told himself

firmly, pacing again. 'But once she knows all the facts
it'll be up to her whether she accepts me or turns me
down. The final decision will be up to her.'

'Jake?' He whirled at the sound of her voice, his
heart melting at the uncertainty he saw in her eyes.
Then she straightened her shoulders as though she,
too, had come to an important decision.

While he watched and waited for her to continue,
her chin tilted up into that endearing don't-mess-with-
me angle and she came across the room until she
stood almost close enough for him to feel the warmth
radiating off her slender body.

'Don't you think it's time we went to bed if we're
going get up in time for work tomorrow?' she asked,
and only the slight quiver in her voice told him that
she wasn't nearly as certain of her reception as she
was pretending.

Maggie saw Jake's eyes widen at her brazen question,
and for a horrible moment wondered if she'd gone
too far. Was he going to reject her out of hand? Then
she saw his pupils dilate in response to her awakening
desire, darkening the sapphire blue to midnight, and
her spirits soared with hope.

'Well, Maggie ffrench!' he exclaimed softly, teasingly, reaching out one hand to smooth back the
strand of hair that had been dishevelled by her recent
bed-making activities. 'If I didn't know better, I'd
think you were propositioning me.'

The proof that he was still her best friend, whatever
else he might become, gave her the courage to tease
him in return.

'And what makes you think I *wasn't* propositioning
you?' she retorted equally softly, not certain whether

David had succumbed to exhausted sleep yet. 'I know after the scare today it wouldn't be a good idea to do anything more than cuddle, but right now I'd settle for that—if you're willing to share your bed?'

She heard Jake draw in a sharp breath, clearly startled by her response, and she suddenly felt the power of her femininity for the first time.

'Of course I'm willing to share my bed with you,' he growled, and everything about him made her think of a force of nature tightly leashed, every muscle tautly straining for the signal to explode into action. 'Did you mean that—about the cuddle?'

For just a second she wondered what on earth she was doing. What had happened to her resolution to put all her cards on the table? She hadn't even told him she loved him, neither had she asked him if there was a chance for them to be together permanently.

But then she looked at him, really looked at the man she knew—the conscientious, driven doctor who chivvied his staff to be the best they could be—and reminded herself that he'd also been gentle and tender with a woman terrified that she'd been losing her baby, the baby they'd created in a night of mutual passion.

Suddenly, nothing else mattered any more. The only thing that really counted was that she had loved Jake ever since she'd met him two years ago and would love him for ever.

'Yes, I mean it,' she whispered, and deliberately walked the last few steps that took her into his arms. 'Take me to bed, please. I need to be with you.'

Any serious conversations could take place when the two of them were well rested and had plenty of time and privacy.

'Ah, Maggie,' he groaned, and she felt the vibrations right through her, every nerve so perfectly tuned to him that it even felt as if they were breathing together. 'You've no idea how difficult it's been, trying to sleep, knowing that you were just a few steps away.'

'I know only too well,' she contradicted. Then, liberated by the knowledge that he wanted to be with her every bit as much as she wanted him, she added, 'I spent all too much time wishing I had the courage to take those few steps to join you.' Then she felt a blush heating her cheeks and realised that perhaps she wasn't quite as liberated as she'd thought.

Jake chuckled as he bent to swing her up into his arms. 'In that case, what are we waiting for? We've got some lost cuddling time to make up for and I've always wanted to do the ''sweep the maiden off her feet'' routine.' He strode into the quiet seclusion of his bedroom and shut the door behind them.

'Maggie? Are you awake?'

She kept her eyes closed but couldn't help smiling as Jake kissed her between each of the words.

'Will you keep kissing me till I wake up?' she murmured, and stretched luxuriously after the best night's sleep she'd had in a long time. Was it just because she'd been so exhausted, or had it been because she'd been wrapped in Jake's arms and lulled by the steady beat of his heart? She didn't even feel sick this morning.

'I'm rather addicted to ffrench kisses myself,' he murmured, and she groaned.

'If I had a pound for every time that joke's been made, I'd be a wealthy woman,' she complained.

'It wouldn't ever happen again if you changed your name,' he suggested softly, his voice suddenly so serious that she opened her eyes and found herself looking straight into intent sapphire blue.

Her peripheral vision was telling her that his body was still as leanly muscled as the first time she'd seen it sprawled out beside her in all its naked glory, but there was something in his expression that wouldn't let her look away.

'Marry me, Maggie,' he said huskily.

Her heart was turning somersaults inside her chest at the thought that he was actually offering her what she'd wanted for two long years, but before she accepted there was one thing she had to know. He hadn't said he loved her, and she wouldn't...*couldn't* accept his proposal if it was only because he'd made her pregnant. After her childhood experience, she would rather bring her child up alone than in a family where it was merely tolerated until it was old enough to be packed off to school.

'Jake, this isn't just about the baby, is it?' she asked, then held her breath while she waited for his reply, knowing all her future happiness depended on it.

'God, Maggie, no!' he exclaimed, apparently stunned that she could even think it. 'I love you and I couldn't care less who the baby's father is. Once we're married it'll be *ours*.'

Maggie was so elated that he'd finally declared his love for her that it took a moment for the rest of his words to register.

'You don't care who the baby's father is?' she repeated in disbelief, then wrenched herself out of his arms, pulling the bedspread around her to cover her modesty and wondering if she was going to be sick after all.

'What do you mean, you don't care who the baby's father is?' She glared at him across the rumpled bed. 'You *know* who the baby's father is.'

He was frowning as he stared at her, apparently puzzled by her anger for a moment, then he rolled out of bed, shaking his head, all the joy completely gone from his face.

'All I know is that it can't be *my* baby,' he said bitterly, and stalked across the room stark naked to grab his dressing-gown off the chair by the door and disappear out into the other room.

CHAPTER TEN

'*WHAT*...do you mean?' Maggie demanded, finishing on a hoarse whisper when she remembered belatedly that David was still asleep.

It hadn't taken her long to grab Jake's discarded shirt and shove her arms into the sleeves. She hadn't paused long enough to fasten the buttons, simply wrapping it around herself and holding it in place with her folded arms so that she could follow him. He couldn't make such a dreadful accusation and storm off without expecting her to defend herself.

'You know damn well that the two of us slept together the night I called off my wedding to Liam,' she reminded him furiously, frustrated that her brother's presence meant she couldn't scream at him like an over-emotional fishwife, the way she wanted to. 'The fact that neither of us remembered to use any protection is one thing, but to imply that I'm no better than a slut...denying that the baby's yours when you're the only man I've ever—' She couldn't continue, her throat closing as she fought the urge to cry.

Jake had been standing in front of the window, staring out as if riveted by the familiar view outside, but now he whirled to face her.

'What *I* know damn well is that your baby *can't* be mine because I'm sterile,' he announced baldly, leaving Maggie gaping at him like a goldfish.

It only took one look at his face to know that this wasn't some clever ploy to try to avoid responsibility

for his actions—Jake honestly believed that he wasn't
the baby's father. She only had to see the pain in his
eyes to know that he was convinced he was telling
the truth.

Her own pain remained, but the anger she'd felt
towards him changed to incomprehension and concern.

'On the other hand,' she said, calmer now that everything began falling into place in her head, '*I* know
that the baby *must* be yours because you're the only
man I've ever slept with. Before or after that night.'

'You... *What*?' It was Jake's turn to be speechless,
the expression on his face changing from disbelief to
hope and back again in as many seconds. 'But...but
you and Liam were engaged. You were getting married the next day. Are you saying...?'

'The *only* man,' she reiterated softly, for once in
her life glad that she'd never wanted to share herself
outside marriage rather than feeling like an out-of-
step throwback to another era. 'So, given that fact,
why don't we sit down calmly and work out where
we go from here?'

She gestured towards the settee, carefully arranging
her skimpy attire to preserve her modesty as she settled into her usual corner.

Moving almost as if he was sleepwalking, Jake
stumbled across and slumped into the other corner,
his eyes never leaving her. It was almost as if he was
afraid that she was going to disappear, like mist in
the morning or an enticing dream that would fade as
soon as he woke.

'Jake...what on earth made you think you were
sterile?' she prompted when he still remained silent,

apparently robbed of the power of speech by the revelations of the last few minutes.

'Chemotherapy,' he croaked, then blinked and cleared his throat.

Maggie couldn't have said a word to save her life. That was the last thing she'd expected. The thought that Jake had suffered—was suffering?—from cancer sent an icy chill down her spine. Had her dearest dream come so close, only to be torn away from her grasp by that most evil of diseases?

'It was diagnosed in my teens…testicular cancer…just before I took my exams,' he continued, the words still slightly disjointed as he put all the facts together for her, but growing more fluent now that he'd started. 'It was the oncologist who told me what the chemo would do to me, but I was just so damn glad that I wasn't going to die that it seemed a fair trade-off at the time.' He smiled briefly. 'Actually, it was spending that time in the hospital that made me want to be a doctor.'

She couldn't imagine what impact a diagnosis like that must have had on a teenager, believing he had a lifetime in front of him only to discover that there was an enormous question mark hanging over it. She could understand that having the future prospect of fatherhood destroyed wouldn't have seemed nearly so important.

'Are you still having treatment?' She hadn't heard any hint of it if he was, and the hospital was a notorious hotbed of gossip.

He shook his head. 'I recently passed my fifteen-year milestone with no recurrence so, no, I'm not on any treatment other than the usual vigilance.'

Maggie allowed herself a silent sigh of relief. At

least Jake's life wasn't in any immediate danger from the disease, but as for their relationship…if they still had a relationship…

'Why didn't you say something…*anything*?' she demanded softly. 'We've known each other for over two years and I thought we were friends. The cancer was something that had a major impact on your life and your future but you never even mentioned—'

'Because I *couldn't*,' he interrupted fiercely, his eyes flashing darkly with remembered disappointment. 'I'd gone that way before with women—the total honesty route—and as soon as they knew that I was sterile it was as if I became a non-person, not even worthy of spending time with any more. So I decided that I was going to adopt a my-career-comes-first attitude, hoping that eventually I'd meet someone who wanted a relationship without the ring and the children to go with it.'

'The handsome playboy consultant,' she teased, remembering that that was what she'd been told about him by the other female staff when she'd first started to work with him. 'So what happened?'

'*You* did.' This time there was heat in his eyes when he looked at her, and her body responded helplessly, her pulse quickening and a shiver of remembered pleasure tightening her skin into sharp sensitivity so that even the thin cotton of his shirt was arousing against her breasts.

'You walked into A and E that first day, all toffee-coloured hair and greeny-blue eyes and legs up to your armpits, so slender and fragile to look at but full of life and grit and determination…and all my plans went out of the window.'

'Why?' How she found the breath to speak even

that much was a miracle. She'd never believed the tales of men being able to seduce with nothing more than the power of words, but she did now.

Thinking back, she knew that she'd fallen in love with Jake almost as soon as she'd set eyes on him. She'd been so disappointed when he hadn't seemed to feel the same attraction, wanting nothing more than friendship from her.

'I fell in love with you almost as soon as I met you,' he said softly. 'I knew that you were the person I wanted—*needed*—for the rest of my life, but before I could do anything, say anything, you were telling me all about the perfect husband and father that you were looking for, and I knew I could never be that person.'

'Oh, Jake… You should have said something because I've spent the last two years wishing *I* could be who *you* wanted. I loved you so much that I would have been only too willing to compromise.'

'But I don't want you to compromise. I wouldn't have wanted you to give up *any* of your dreams,' he objected. 'You deserve to have all the good things.'

'And we could have,' she pointed out, 'unless you've got some objection to adopting?'

'No, none, but—' He broke off and shook his head. 'Oh, why are we bothering discussing this when it's a moot point? You're already pregnant.'

'Well, I had hoped to have more than one child,' she pointed out, a sudden bubble of excitement rising inside her when she realised that he'd tacitly accepted that the baby was his. She stroked a tender hand over the disappointing flatness of her stomach, suddenly eager for the day when the evidence of the child growing there would be plain for all to see. 'We don't know whether this one was a miraculous one-off, or whether your system was able to withstand the chemical bombardment better than the oncologist predicted. That is…if *you* want more than one child?'

'Oh, God, Maggie, come here!' He reached out across the settee towards her and she scrambled across the intervening distance and into his arms, almost giddy with happiness. 'Anything and everything,' he muttered into her hair. His arms were wrapped tightly around her, their bodies joined together so closely they could have been two halves of a whole that had finally been reunited. 'You can have as many children as you want—our own or adopted— as long as you love me.'

'Always, Jake,' she promised, already tilting her head to invite his kiss.

He held back, even though she could feel from the tension in every nerve and sinew that he wanted to taste her lips.

'And you'll marry me, Maggie?'

Was that a lingering hint of uncertainty she heard? If so, it needed to be dispelled once and for all.

'Of course I will, Jake. As soon as you like.' She threaded her fingers through his hair and pulled him down to meet her urgent kiss.

Desire exploded between them, the detonation shaking her whole world as she knew for the first time that she was truly loved. Jake surfaced briefly, apparently every bit as shaken by the depth of emotion they now shared, his dark blue eyes almost feral in their need to possess.

'Take me back to bed?' she suggested, almost embarrassed by her eagerness. All she had to do was look in his eyes to see that he wanted to take their desire to its logical conclusion, too.

'We can't,' he groaned, dropping his head back against the cushions even as he tightened his hold on her. 'There isn't time before we have to get ready for work.' He drew a tender finger down the side of her face, then on to her throat, where he paused as though testing her racing pulse.

'Anyway, as your doctor, I'd recommend waiting a couple of days after the scare you had yesterday. As your frustrated lover and husband-to-be…I just want to carry you off to bed and ravish you.' He cradled her face in his hand, stroking a loving fingertip over her kiss-swollen lips. She parted them, teasing the tip of his finger with her tongue and smiling wickedly at his groaned response.

'Moggie, what time is it?' David demanded as he stumbled blearily out into the sitting room. 'I forgot to change the time on my watch before I landed and I'm still on New Zealand— Oops!' His rambling monologue came to an abrupt end.

'Just opened your eyes?' she asked, without bothering to look in his direction. She was far more interested in looking at Jake than her jet-lagged brother, while Jake was chivalrously straightening her borrowed shirt so it preserved a little more of her modesty.

'I—I'm sorry, Moggie… Jake,' David stammered. 'I'll just…go away.' She was tempted to giggle at the obvious embarrassment in his halting speech.

'Don't go,' Jake said, apparently taking pity on a fellow male. 'You can be the first to congratulate me. Your sister's going to make an honest man of me.'

'Oh?' David sounded puzzled for a moment, and

Maggie smiled, realising that in all probability his brain was still half-asleep.

'Oh!' he exclaimed as the penny finally dropped. 'Congratulations! But are you sure you know what you're taking on? Surely I told you enough about her last night to put you off the idea?'

Maggie shared a besotted look with Jake and then they both looked back at David, shaking their heads.

For just a moment Maggie thought she saw an expression of pain in her brother's eyes, but then he blinked and whatever it was had gone. All her instincts suddenly told her that his trip 'home' was something other than a pleasant visit, that something untoward had happened in New Zealand, but this was neither the time nor the place to find out.

'Ah, well, no one can say I didn't at least try to warn you off the idea,' David said mournfully, a definite edge to his voice as he turned back the way he'd come. 'It's sad to see another good man ruined by marriage.' He waved dismissively over his shoulder as he disappeared, his voice floating back to them. 'You might as well get back to...whatever you were doing.'

'ffrench kissing!' Maggie supplied with a giggle, and David groaned and shut the door with a resounding click. 'Now, where were we?' she said, smiling in anticipation at carrying on where she and Jake had left off when her brother had so rudely interrupted them. 'Ah, yes. Practising our ffrench kissing.'

'Don't tempt me,' Jake pleaded. 'Not when we've got to be at work in less than an hour.'

He went to put her away from him and she lost her precarious hold on the edges of the shirt, allowing him more than a glimpse of what it had concealed.

'Ah, Maggie,' he breathed, and she saw the fine tremor in his hand as he reached out to trace her curves. 'Perfection.'

After several minutes of sharply increased heart-beat on both their parts he managed to call a halt, and even then he returned to her lips for a final kiss.

'You know, that's what I'm looking forward to,' he said huskily, burying his face in the exposed angle between her neck and shoulder. 'That last ffrench kiss.'

'The last kiss?' Maggie was puzzled.

'The last *ffrench* kiss,' he corrected with a glimpse of his trade-mark grin. 'When you change your name from ffrench to Lascelles.'

'But that's French, too,' she pointed out logically, finally having to accept that there was no more time to dally and extricating herself from his lap. 'So instead of a last ffrench kiss we can look forward to a lifetime of...French kisses!'

'Ooh, that hurts!' Maggie moaned as soon as she took the hand-held mask away from her sweaty face, panting in the aftermath of a massive contraction.

'Not far to go, now, my love,' Jake consoled her as he wiped her face with a cool cloth and offered her a sip of icy cold water.

'What do you mean, not far to go?' she snapped, glaring at him malevolently. 'I've been going through this agony for days and all you can say is *Not far to go*—as if *you've* been doing any of the work. You were only there for the first five minutes, nine months ago. Well, let me tell you, just because you've got a supersonic sperm count doesn't mean that I'm going to be going through this again in a hurry— Ah-h! Not another contraction already!'

Maggie slapped the mask back over her face and drew in a deep lungful of gas and air, then tried to release it in a calm, controlled stream. But calm and controlled wasn't working any more. She just wanted to scream or hit something…hard!

'Transition,' she heard the midwife mutter in an aside to Jake, even as a tiny rational corner of Maggie's brain was telling her that ranting at the poor man wasn't helping the situation. He had been so caring and considerate right through her pregnancy that he certainly didn't deserve it.

But then the wave of pain intensified still further, and all she could concentrate on was what her body was having to suffer and whether she could possibly survive it.

'And you can forget about any more children,' she croaked when she caught her breath after the baby's latest attempt to wrench her in half. She grimaced when, out of the corner of her eye, she saw the midwife donning a fresh pair of gloves. She really hated having those periodic examinations.

'If you want any more, *you* can carry the next one and give birth to it,' she snapped, wondering how on earth he could bear to look at her so lovingly when her face was red and sweaty, her hair was lank and sweaty and her body was enormously misshapen… and sweaty. 'Then you'll see what it's like to waddle around like a hippopotamus for months on end and then have to suffer agonising pain for hours on end and—'

'Hush, Maggie, and save your breath,' Jake said gently, apparently totally unconcerned by her nasty tongue or anything else other than being there for her as she gave birth to their child. 'It's time to push.'

'I don't *want* to push,' she argued through gritted teeth, hating the feeling that everything was out of her control. '*You* push if you want to. I just want to go home and forget all about having— Ooh, Jake, I've got to push...*now*!'

'Oh, Maggie, thank you,' Jake murmured as he gazed down at the tiny bundle cradled in his arms. He took the single step that separated the clear plastic cot from her bed to settle himself comfortably beside the woman who was the whole world to him.

It didn't take much manoeuvring to slip his arm around her slender shoulders so that they were both cradling their child, and his heart swelled at the way she automatically leant her head on his shoulder.

'She's perfect,' Maggie whispered, and he watched her reach out a tender finger to trace the curve of baby Megan's head, then linger to smooth the dark hair she'd inherited from him. They knew that it was too soon to tell which of them she'd follow with her eye colour, but he decided that her petite features and elegant fingers belonged to Maggie.

'As perfect as her mother,' he said with a full heart, then pressed a kiss to her freshly washed hair.

He smiled, thinking of her insistence that she couldn't bear to stay so sweaty a moment longer once she'd been brought to her room from the delivery suite. She'd probably have fought him to a standstill if he'd tried to stop her getting into the shower rather than helping her feel fresh and clean again. As if he cared about the state of her hair when she'd just given him the gift he'd never thought to have—a child of his own.

Megan chose that moment to stretch and open her eyes, almost immediately beginning to voice her demands for the next meal.

With the self-conscious expertise of new parents they transferred the squalling bundle to Maggie's arms and within moments the room was filled with the gentle sound of contented suckling.

Jake didn't think he could ever get tired of that sight. Maggie and Megan made the perfect picture, reminiscent of the Madonna and Child painted by so many great artists. The best part was that these were so much more than a clever illusion of paint on canvas; they were flesh and blood and they were forever a part of him.

'Jake, I've been thinking,' Maggie said in a musing voice, and when she looked up at him with what he thought of as her 'wheedling' face all his instincts went on alert.

It was just such a look that had persuaded him that they could organise the perfect wedding in less than a month—including contacting Taff and arranging for his choir to sing for them. That was now nearly six months ago, but he still shuddered when he remembered the multitude of things that had needed co-ordinating before he'd finally been able to place his ring on her finger.

'What have you been thinking about?' he asked warily, grateful that at least he should be spared any more midnight runs to the nearest all-night shop to satisfy some outlandish craving.

'Well, a pregnancy lasts for nine months, give or take a few days, and that's a very long time.'

'Yes,' he agreed guardedly. He could have reminded her that she'd been metaphorically beating him over the head with those facts just a short while ago, when she'd been in that hormone hell known as transition. He didn't.

'Well, what I was thinking was…' She glanced up at him so innocently that he had absolutely no idea what was coming next, and he was holding his breath when she continued. 'Everybody says that babies grow up so fast, and as it takes so long to have them, how soon do you think we can get started on another one?'

He burst out laughing.

'Ah, Maggie! I love you!' he exclaimed, his heart full enough to burst with love for this amazing woman.

They both knew that her body needed time to recover from its recent ordeal, but the fact that she was already looking forward to bearing another child was a testimony to her indomitable spirit.

Even so, her question was an easy one to answer.

'As soon as you want to, Maggie, my love,' he promised, and she looked up at him with a happy smile. 'But,' he temporised in a whispered aside, 'just so we don't scandalise all the A and E staff waiting to come in and visit, could we wait until we get home?'

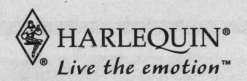
HARLEQUIN®
Live the emotion™

AMERICAN *Romance*®

Upbeat,
All-American Romances

flipside

Romantic Comedy

Harlequin Historicals®

Historical,
Romantic Adventure

INTRIGUE

Romantic Suspense

HARLEQUIN ROMANCE®

The essence of
modern romance

HARLEQUIN®
Presents

Seduction and passion
guaranteed

HARLEQUIN® *Super*ROMANCE®

Emotional,
Exciting, Unexpected

Temptation.

Sassy, Sexy, Seductive!

eHARLEQUIN.com

The Ultimate Destination for Women's Fiction

The eHarlequin.com online community is *the* place to share opinions, thoughts and feelings!

- Joining the community is easy, fun and **FREE!**

- Connect with **other romance fans** on our message boards.

- Meet your **favorite authors** without leaving home!

- **Share opinions** on books, movies, celebrities…and *more!*

Here's what our members say:

"I love the friendly and helpful atmosphere filled with support and humor."
—Texanna (eHarlequin.com member)

"Is this the place for me, or what? There is nothing I love more than 'talking' books, especially with fellow readers who are reading the same ones I am."
—Jo Ann (eHarlequin.com member)

Join today by visiting www.eHarlequin.com!

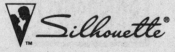